The Second Part of Henry the Fourth

William Shakespeare

MAPLE PRESS

THE SECOND PART OF HENRY THE FOURTH by William Shakespeare

Published by

MAPLE PRESS PRIVATE LIMITED
office: A-63, Sector 58, Noida 201301, U.P., India
phone: +91 120 455 3581, 455 3583
email: info@maplepress.co.in
website: www.maplepress.co.in
Go to www.maplelibrary.com for more e-books.

Reprinted in 2019
Printed and bound in Noida, India

ISBN: 978-93-50334-39-3

Contents

INDUCTION

Warkworth. Before the castle

Enter Rumour, painted full of tongues

Rumour: Open your ears; for which of you will stop
The vent of hearing when loud Rumour speaks?
I, from the orient to the drooping west,
Making the wind my post-horse, still unfold
The acts commenced on this ball of earth:
Upon my tongues continual slanders ride,
The which in every language I pronounce,
Stuffing the ears of men with false reports.
I speak of peace, while covert enmity
Under the smile of safety wounds the world:
And who but Rumour, who but only I,
Make fearful musters and prepared defence,
Whiles the big year, swoln with some other grief,
Is thought with child by the stern tyrant war,
And no such matter? Rumour is a pipe
Blown by surmises, jealousies, conjectures
And of so easy and so plain a stop
That the blunt monster with uncounted heads,
The still-discordant wavering multitude,
Can play upon it. But what need I thus
My well-known body to anatomize
Among my household? Why is Rumour here?
I run before King Harry's victory;
Who in a bloody field by Shrewsbury

Hath beaten down young Hotspur and his troops,
Quenching the flame of bold rebellion
Even with the rebel's blood. But what mean I
To speak so true at first? my office is
To noise abroad that Harry Monmouth fell
Under the wrath of noble Hotspur's sword,
And that the king before the Douglas' rage
Stoop'd his anointed head as low as death.
This have I Rumour'd through the peasant towns
Between that royal field of Shrewsbury
And this worm-eaten hold of ragged stone,
Where Hotspur's father, old Northumberland,
Lies crafty-sick: the posts come tiring on,
And not a man of them brings other news
Than they have learn'd of me: from Rumour's tongues
They bring smooth comforts false, worse than
true wrongs.

Exit

ACT I

SCENE I

The same

Enter Lord Bardolph

Lord Bardolph: Who keeps the gate here, ho?

The Porter opens the gate

Where is the earl?

Porter: What shall I say you are?

Lord Bardolph: Tell thou the earl
That the Lord Bardolph doth attend him here.

Porter: His lordship is walk'd forth into the orchard;
Please it your honour, knock but at the gate,
And he himself wilt answer.

Enter Northumberland

Lord Bardolph: Here comes the earl.

Exit Porter

Northumberland: What news, Lord Bardolph? every minute now
Should be the father of some stratagem:
The times are wild: contention, like a horse
Full of high feeding, madly hath broke loose
And bears down all before him.

Lord Bardolph: Noble earl,
I bring you certain news from Shrewsbury.

Northumberland: Good, an God will!

Lord Bardolph: As good as heart can wish:
The king is almost wounded to the death;
And, in the fortune of my lord your son,
Prince Harry slain outright; and both the Blunts

Kill'd by the hand of Douglas; young Prince John
And Westmoreland and Stafford fled the field;
And Harry Monmouth's brawn, the hulk Sir John,
Is prisoner to your son: O, such a day,
So fought, so follow'd and so fairly won,
Came not till now to dignify the times,
Since Caesar's fortunes!

Northumberland: How is this derived?
Saw you the field? came you from Shrewsbury?

Lord Bardolph: I spake with one, my lord, that came from thence,
A gentleman well bred and of good name,
That freely render'd me these news for true.

Northumberland: Here comes my servant Travers, whom I sent
On Tuesday last to listen after news.

Enter Travers

Lord Bardolph: My lord, I over-rode him on the way;
And he is furnish'd with no certainties
More than he haply may retail from me.

Northumberland: Now, Travers, what good tidings comes with you?

Travers: My lord, Sir John Umfrevile turn'd me back
With joyful tidings; and, being better horsed,
Out-rode me. After him came spurring hard
A gentleman, almost forspent with speed,
That stopp'd by me to breathe his bloodied horse.
He ask'd the way to Chester; and of him
I did demand what news from Shrewsbury:
He told me that rebellion had bad luck
And that young Harry Percy's spur was cold.
With that, he gave his able horse the head,

And bending forward struck his armed heels
Against the panting sides of his poor jade
Up to the rowel-head, and starting so
He seem'd in running to devour the way,
Staying no longer question.

Northumberland: Ha! Again:
Said he young Harry Percy's spur was cold?
Of Hotspur Coldspur? that rebellion
Had met ill luck?

Lord Bardolph: My lord, I'll tell you what;
If my young lord your son have not the day,
Upon mine honour, for a silken point
I'll give my barony: never talk of it.

Northumberland: Why should that gentleman that rode by Travers
Give then such instances of loss?

Lord Bardolph: Who, he?
He was some hilding fellow that had stolen
The horse he rode on, and, upon my life,
Spoke at a venture. Look, here comes more news.

Enter Morton

Northumberland: Yea, this man's brow, like to a title-leaf,
Foretells the nature of a tragic volume:
So looks the strand whereon the imperious flood
Hath left a witness'd usurpation.
Say, Morton, didst thou come from Shrewsbury?

Morton: I ran from Shrewsbury, my noble lord;
Where hateful death put on his ugliest mask
To fright our party.

Northumberland: How doth my son and brother?
Thou tremblest; and the whiteness in thy cheek

Is apter than thy tongue to tell thy errand.
Even such a man, so faint, so spiritless,
So dull, so dead in look, so woe-begone,
Drew Priam's curtain in the dead of night,
And would have told him half his Troy was burnt;
But Priam found the fire ere he his tongue,
And I my Percy's death ere thou report'st it.
This thou wouldst say, 'Your son did thus and thus;
Your brother thus: so fought the noble Douglas:'
Stopping my greedy ear with their bold deeds:
But in the end, to stop my ear indeed,
Thou hast a sigh to blow away this praise,
Ending with 'Brother, son, and all are dead.'

Morton: Douglas is living, and your brother, yet;
But, for my lord your son-

Northumberland: Why, he is dead.
See what a ready tongue suspicion hath!
He that but fears the thing he would not know
Hath by instinct knowledge from others' eyes
That what he fear'd is chanced. Yet speak, Morton;
Tell thou an earl his divination lies,
And I will take it as a sweet disgrace
And make thee rich for doing me such wrong.

Morton: You are too great to be by me gainsaid:
Your spirit is too true, your fears too certain.

Northumberland: Yet, for all this, say not that Percy's dead.
I see a strange confession in thine eye:
Thou shakest thy head and hold'st it fear or sin
To speak a truth. If he be slain, say so;
The tongue offends not that reports his death:

And he doth sin that doth belie the dead,
Not he which says the dead is not alive.
Yet the first bringer of unwelcome news
Hath but a losing office, and his tongue
Sounds ever after as a sullen bell,
Remember'd tolling a departing friend.

Lord Bardolph: I cannot think, my lord, your son is dead.

Morton: I am sorry I should force you to believe
That which I would to God I had not seen;
But these mine eyes saw him in bloody state,
Rendering faint quittance, wearied and out-breathed,
To Harry Monmouth; whose swift wrath beat down
The never-daunted Percy to the earth,
From whence with life he never more sprung up.
In few, his death, whose spirit lent a fire
Even to the dullest peasant in his camp,
Being bruited once, took fire and heat away
From the best temper'd courage in his troops;
For from his metal was his party steel'd;
Which once in him abated, all the rest
Turn'd on themselves, like dull and heavy lead:
And as the thing that's heavy in itself,
Upon enforcement flies with greatest speed,
So did our men, heavy in Hotspur's loss,
Lend to this weight such lightness with their fear
That arrows fled not swifter toward their aim
Than did our soldiers, aiming at their safety,
Fly from the field. Then was the noble Worcester
Too soon ta'en prisoner; and that furious Scot,
The bloody Douglas, whose well-labouring sword

Had three times slain the appearance of the king,
'Gan vail his stomach and did grace the shame
Of those that turn'd their backs, and in his flight,
Stumbling in fear, was took. The sum of all
Is that the king hath won, and hath sent out
A speedy power to encounter you, my lord,
Under the conduct of young Lancaster
And Westmoreland. This is the news at full.

Northumberland: For this I shall have time enough to mourn.
In poison there is physic; and these news,
Having been well, that would have made me sick,
Being sick, have in some measure made me well:
And as the wretch, whose fever-weaken'd joints,
Like strengthless hinges, buckle under life,
Impatient of his fit, breaks like a fire
Out of his keeper's arms, even so my limbs,
Weaken'd with grief, being now enraged with grief,
Are thrice themselves. Hence, therefore, thou nice crutch!
A scaly gauntlet now with joints of steel
Must glove this hand: and hence, thou sickly quoif!
Thou art a guard too wanton for the head
Which princes, flesh'd with conquest, aim to hit.
Now bind my brows with iron; and approach
The ragged'st hour that time and spite dare bring
To frown upon the enraged Northumberland!
Let heaven kiss earth! now let not Nature's hand
Keep the wild flood confined! let order die!
And let this world no longer be a stage
To feed contention in a lingering act;

But let one spirit of the first-born Cain
Reign in all bosoms, that, each heart being set
On bloody courses, the rude scene may end,
And darkness be the burier of the dead!

Travers: This strained passion doth you wrong, my lord.

Lord Bardolph: Sweet earl, divorce not wisdom from your honour.

Morton: The lives of all your loving complices
Lean on your health; the which, if you give o'er
To stormy passion, must perforce decay.
You cast the event of war, my noble lord,
And summ'd the account of chance, before you said
'Let us make head.' It was your presurmise,
That, in the dole of blows, your son might drop:
You knew he walk'd o'er perils, on an edge,
More likely to fall in than to get o'er;
You were advised his flesh was capable
Of wounds and scars and that his forward spirit
Would lift him where most trade of danger ranged:
Yet did you say 'Go forth;' and none of this,
Though strongly apprehended, could restrain
The stiff-borne action: what hath then befallen,
Or what hath this bold enterprise brought forth,
More than that being which was like to be?

Lord Bardolph: We all that are engaged to this loss
Knew that we ventured on such dangerous seas
That if we wrought our life 'twas ten to one;
And yet we ventured, for the gain proposed
Choked the respect of likely peril fear'd;
And since we are o'erset, venture again.
Come, we will all put forth, body and goods.

Morton: 'Tis more than time: and, my most noble lord,
I hear for certain, and do speak the truth,
The gentle Archbishop of York is up
With well-appointed powers: he is a man
Who with a double surety binds his followers.
My lord your son had only but the corpse,
But shadows and the shows of men, to fight;
For that same word, rebellion, did divide
The action of their bodies from their souls;
And they did fight with queasiness, constrain'd,
As men drink potions, that their weapons only
Seem'd on our side; but, for their spirits and souls,
This word, rebellion, it had froze them up,
As fish are in a pond. But now the bishop
Turns insurrecti on to religion:
Supposed sincere and holy in his thoughts,
He's followed both with body and with mind;
And doth enlarge his rising with the blood
Of fair King Richard, scraped from Pomfret stones;
Derives from heaven his quarrel and his cause;
Tells them he doth bestride a bleeding land,
Gasping for life under great Bolingbroke;
And more and less do flock to follow him.

Northumberland: I knew of this before; but, to speak truth,
This present grief had wiped it from my mind.
Go in with me; and counsel every man
The aptest way for safety and revenge:
Get posts and letters, and make friends with speed:
Never so few, and never yet more need.

Exeunt

SCENE II

London. A street

Enter Falstaff, with his Page bearing his sword and buckler

Falstaff: Sirrah, you giant, what says the doctor to my water?

Page: He said, sir, the water itself was a good healthy water; but, for the party that owed it, he might have more diseases than he knew for.

Falstaff: Men of all sorts take a pride to gird at me: the brain of this foolish-compounded clay, man, is not able to invent anything that tends to laughter, more than I invent or is invented on me: I am not only witty in myself, but the cause that wit is in other men. I do here walk before thee like a sow that hath overwhelmed all her litter but one. If the prince put thee into my service for any other reason than to set me off, why then I have no judgment. Thou whoreson mandrake, thou art fitter to be worn in my cap than to wait at my heels. I was never manned with an agate till now: but I will inset you neither in gold nor silver, but in vile apparel, and send you back again to your master, for a jewel,- the juvenal, the prince your master, whose chin is not yet fledged. I will sooner have a beard grow in the palm of my hand than he shall get one on his cheek; and yet he will not stick to say his face is a face-royal: God may finish it when he will, 'tis not a hair amiss yet: he may keep it still at a face-royal, for a barber shall never earn sixpence out of it; and yet he'll be crowing as if he had writ man ever since his father was a bachelor. He may keep his own grace, but he's almost out of mine, I can assure him. What said Master Dombledon about the satin for my short cloak and my slops?

Page: He said, sir, you should procure him better assurance than Bardolph: he would not take his band and yours; he liked not the security.

Falstaff: Let him be damned, like the glutton! pray God his tongue be hotter! A whoreson Achitophel! a rascally yea-forsooth knave! to bear a gentleman in hand, and then stand upon security! The whoreson smooth-pates do now wear nothing but high shoes, and bunches of keys at their girdles; and if a man is through with them in honest taking up, then they must stand upon security. I had as lief they would put ratsbane in my mouth as offer to stop it with security. I looked a' should have sent me two and twenty yards of satin, as I am a true knight, and he sends me security. Well, he may sleep in security; for he hath the horn of abundance, and the lightness of his wife shines through it: and yet cannot he see, though he have his own lanthorn to light him. Where's Bardolph?

Page: He's gone into Smithfield to buy your worship a horse.

Falstaff: I bought him in Paul's, and he'll buy me a horse in Smithfield: an I could get me but a wife in the stews, I were manned, horsed, and wived.

Enter the Lord Chief-Justice and Servant

Page: Sir, here comes the nobleman that committed the Prince for striking him about Bardolph.

Falstaff: Wait, close; I will not see him.

Lord Chief-Justice: What's he that goes there?

Servant: Falstaff, an't please your lordship.

Lord Chief-Justice: He that was in question for the robbery?

Servant: He, my lord: but he hath since done good service at Shrewsbury; and, as I hear, is now going with some charge to the Lord John of Lancaster.

Lord Chief-Justice: What, to York? Call him back again.

Servant: Sir John Falstaff!

Falstaff: Boy, tell him I am deaf.

Page: You must speak louder; my master is deaf.

Lord Chief-Justice: I am sure he is, to the hearing of anything good. Go, pluck him by the elbow; I must speak with him.

Servant: Sir John!

Falstaff: What! a young knave, and begging! Is there not wars? is there not employment? doth not the king lack subjects? do not the rebels need soldiers? Though it be a shame to be on any side but one, it is worse shame to beg than to be on the worst side, were it worse than the name of rebellion can tell how to make it.

Servant: You mistake me, sir.

Falstaff: Why, sir, did I say you were an honest man? setting my knighthood and my soldiership aside, I had lied in my throat, if I had said so.

Servant: I pray you, sir, then set your knighthood and our

soldiership aside; and give me leave to tell you, you lie in your throat, if you say I am any other than an honest man.

Falstaff: I give thee leave to tell me so! I lay aside that which grows to me! if thou gettest any leave of me, hang me; if thou takest leave, thou wert better be hanged. You hunt counter: hence! avaunt!

Servant: Sir, my lord would speak with you.

Lord Chief-Justice: Sir John Falstaff, a word with you.

Falstaff: My good lord! God give your lordship good time of day. I am glad to see your lordship abroad: I heard say your lordship was sick: I hope your lordship goes abroad by advice. Your lordship, though not clean past your youth, hath yet some smack of age in you, some relish of the saltness of time; and I must humbly beseech your lordship to have a reverent care of your health.

Lord Chief-Justice: Sir John, I sent for you before your expedition to Shrewsbury.

Falstaff: An't please your lordship, I hear his majesty is returned with some discomfort from Wales.

Lord Chief-Justice: I talk not of his majesty: you would not come when I sent for you.

Falstaff: And I hear, moreover, his highness is fallen into this same whoreson apoplexy.

Lord Chief-Justice: Well, God mend him! I pray you, let me speak with you.

Falstaff: This apoplexy is, as I take it, a kind of lethargy, an't please your lordship; a kind of sleeping in the blood, a whoreson tingling.

Lord Chief-Justice: What tell you me of it? be it as it is.

Falstaff: It hath its original from much grief, from study and perturbation of the brain: I have read the cause of his effects in Galen: it is a kind of deafness.

Lord Chief-Justice: I think you are fallen into the disease; for you hear not what I say to you.

Falstaff: Very well, my lord, very well: rather, an't please you, it is the disease of not listening, the malady of not marking, that I am troubled withal.

Lord Chief-Justice: To punish you by the heels would amend the attention of your ears; and I care not if I do become your physician.

Falstaff: I am as poor as Job, my lord, but not so patient: your lordship may minister the potion of imprisonment to me in respect of poverty; but how should I be your patient to follow your prescriptions, the wise may make some dram of a scruple, or indeed a scruple itself.

Lord Chief-Justice: I sent for you, when there were matters against you for your life, to come speak with me.

Falstaff: As I was then advised by my learned counsel in the laws of this land-service, I did not come.

Lord Chief-Justice: Well, the truth is, Sir John, you live in great infamy.

Falstaff: He that buckles him in my belt cannot live in less.

Lord Chief-Justice: Your means are very slender, and your waste is great.

Falstaff: I would it were otherwise; I would my means were greater, and my waist slenderer.

Lord Chief-Justice: You have misled the youthful prince.

Falstaff: The young prince hath misled me: I am the fellow with the great belly, and he my dog.

Lord Chief-Justice: Well, I am loath to gall a new-healed wound: your day's service at Shrewsbury hath a little gilded over your night's exploit on Gad's-hill: you may thank the unquiet time for your quiet o'er-posting that action.

Falstaff: My lord?

Lord Chief-Justice: But since all is well, keep it so: wake not a sleeping wolf.

Falstaff: To wake a wolf is as bad as to smell a fox.

Lord Chief-Justice: What! you are as a candle, the better part burnt out.

Falstaff: A wassail candle, my lord, all tallow: if I did say of wax, my growth would approve the truth.

Lord Chief-Justice: There is not a white hair on your face but should have his effect of gravity.

Falstaff: His effect of gravy, gravy, gravy.

Lord Chief-Justice: You follow the young prince up and down, like his ill angel.

Falstaff: Not so, my lord; your ill angel is light; but I hope he that looks upon me will take me without weighing: and yet, in some respects, I grant, I cannot go: I cannot tell. Virtue is of so little regard in these costermonger times that true valour is turned bear-herd: pregnancy is made a tapster, and hath his quick wit wasted in giving reckonings: all the other gifts appertinent to man, as the malice of this age shapes them, are not worth a gooseberry. You that are old consider not the capacities of us that are young; you do measure the heat of our livers with the bitterness of your galls: and we that are in the vaward of our youth, I must confess, are wags too.

Lord Chief-Justice: Do you set down your name in the scroll of youth, that are written down old with all the characters of age? Have you not a moist eye? a dry hand? a yellow cheek? a white beard? a decreasing leg? an increasing belly? is not your voice broken? your wind short? your chin double? your wit single? and every part about you blasted with antiquity? and will you yet call yourself young? Fie, fie, fie, Sir John!

Falstaff: My lord, I was born about three of the clock in the afternoon, with a white head and something a round belly. For my voice, I have lost it with halloing and singing of anthems. To approve my youth further, I will not: the truth is, I am only old in judgment and understanding; and he that will caper with me for a thousand marks, let him lend me the money, and have at him! For the box of the ear that the prince gave you, he gave it like a rude prince, and you took it like a sensible lord. I have chequed him for it, and the young lion repents; marry, not in ashes and sackcloth, but in new silk and old sack.

Lord Chief-Justice: Well, God send the prince a better companion!

Falstaff: God send the companion a better prince! I cannot rid my hands of him.

Lord Chief-Justice: Well, the king hath severed you and Prince Harry:I hear you are going with Lord John of Lancaster against the Archbishop and the Earl of Northumberland.

Falstaff: Yea; I thank your pretty sweet wit for it. But look you pray, all you that kiss my lady Peace at home, that our armies join not in a hot day; for, by the Lord, I take but two shirts out with me, and I mean not to sweat extraordinarily: if it be a hot day, and I brandish anything but a bottle, I would I might never spit white again. There is not a dangerous action can peep out his head but I am thrust upon it: well, I cannot last ever: but it was alway yet the trick of our English nation, if they have a good thing, to make it too common. If ye will needs say I am an old man, you should give me rest. I would to God my name were not so terrible to the enemy as it is: I were better to be eaten to death with a rust than to be scoured to nothing with perpetual motion.

Lord Chief-Justice: Well, be honest, be honest; and God bless your expedition!

Falstaff: Will your lordship lend me a thousand pound to furnish me forth?

Lord Chief-Justice: Not a penny, not a penny; you are too impatient to bear crosses. Fare you well: commend me to my cousin Westmoreland.

Exeunt Chief-Justice and Servant

Falstaff: If I do, fillip me with a three-man beetle. A man can no more separate age and covetousness than a' can part young limbs and lechery: but the gout galls the one, and the pox pinches the other; and so both the degrees prevent my curses. Boy!

Page: Sir?

Falstaff: What money is in my purse?

Page: Seven groats and two pence.

Falstaff: I can get no remedy against this consumption of the purse: borrowing only lingers and lingers it out, but the disease is incurable. Go bear this letter to my Lord of Lancaster; this to the prince; this to the Earl of Westmoreland; and this to old Mistress Ursula, whom I have weekly sworn to marry since I perceived the first white hair on my chin. About it: you know where to find me.

Exit Page

A pox of this gout! or, a gout of this pox! for the one or the other plays the rogue with my great toe. 'Tis no matter if I do halt; I have the wars for my colour, and my pension shall seem the more reasonable. A good wit will make use of any thing: I will turn diseases to commodity.

Exit

SCENE III

York. The Archbishop's palace

Enter the Archbishop of York, the Lords Hastings, Mowbray, and Bardolph

Archbishop of York: Thus have you heard our cause and known our means;
And, my most noble friends, I pray you all,
Speak plainly your opinions of our hopes:
And first, lord marshal, what say you to it?

Mowbray: I well allow the occasion of our arms;
But gladly would be better satisfied
How in our means we should advance ourselves
To look with forehead bold and big enough
Upon the power and puissance of the king.

Hastings: Our present musters grow upon the file
To five and twenty thousand men of choice;
And our supplies live largely in the hope
Of great Northumberland, whose bosom burns
With an incensed fire of injuries.

Lord Bardolph: The question then, Lord Hastings, standeth thus;
Whether our present five and twenty thousand
May hold up head without Northumberland?

Hastings: With him, we may.

Lord Bardolph: Yea, marry, there's the point:
But if without him we be thought too Feeble,
My judgment is, we should not step too far
Till we had his assistance by the hand;
For in a theme so bloody-faced as this

Conjecture, expectation, and surmise
Of aids incertain should not be admitted.

Archbishop of York: 'Tis very true, Lord Bardolph; for indeed
It was young Hotspur's case at Shrewsbury.

Lord Bardolph: It was, my lord; who lined himself with hope,
Eating the air on promise of supply,
Flattering himself in project of a power
Much smaller than the smallest of his thoughts:
And so, with great imagination
Proper to madmen, led his powers to death
And winking leap'd into destruction.

Hastings: But, by your leave, it never yet did hurt
To lay down likelihoods and forms of hope.

Lord Bardolph: Yes, if this present quality of war,
Indeed the instant action: a cause on foot
Lives so in hope as in an early spring
We see the appearing buds; which to prove fruit,
Hope gives not so much warrant as despair
That frosts will bite them. When we mean to build,
We first survey the plot, then draw the model;
And when we see the figure of the house,
Then must we rate the cost of the erection;
Which if we find outweighs ability,
What do we then but draw anew the model
In fewer offices, or at last desist
To build at all? Much more, in this great work,
Which is almost to pluck a kingdom down
And set another up, should we survey
The plot of situation and the model,
Consent upon a sure foundation,

Question surveyors, know our own estate,
How able such a work to undergo,
To weigh against his opposite; or else
We fortify in paper and in figures,
Using the names of men instead of men:
Like one that draws the model of a house
Beyond his power to build it; who, half through,
Gives o'er and leaves his part-created cost
A naked subject to the weeping clouds
And waste for churlish winter's tyranny.

Hastings: Grant that our hopes, yet likely of fair birth,
Should be still-born, and that we now possess'd
The utmost man of expectation,
I think we are a body strong enough,
Even as we are, to equal with the king.

Lord Bardolph: What, is the king but five and twenty thousand?

Hastings: To us no more; nay, not so much, Lord Bardolph.
For his divisions, as the times do brawl,
Are in three heads: one power against the French,
And one against Glendower; perforce a third
Must take up us: so is the unfirm king
In three divided; and his coffers sound
With hollow poverty and emptiness.

Archbishop of York: That he should draw his several strengths together
And come against us in full puissance,
Need not be dreaded.

Hastings: If he should do so,
He leaves his back unarm'd, the French and Welsh
Baying him at the heels: never fear that.

Lord Bardolph: Who is it like should lead his forces hither?

Hastings: The Duke of Lancaster and Westmoreland;

Against the Welsh, himself and Harry Monmouth:
But who is substituted 'gainst the French,
I have no certain notice.

Archbishop of York: Let us on,
And publish the occasion of our arms.
The commonwealth is sick of their own choice;
Their over-greedy love hath surfeited:
An habitation giddy and unsure
Hath he that buildeth on the vulgar heart.
O thou fond many, with what loud applause
Didst thou beat heaven with blessing Bolingbroke,
Before he was what thou wouldst have him be!
And being now trimm'd in thine own desires,
Thou, beastly feeder, art so full of him,
That thou provokest thyself to cast him up.
So, so, thou common dog, didst thou disgorge
Thy glutton bosom of the royal Richard;
And now thou wouldst eat thy dead vomit up,
And howl'st to find it. What trust is in
these times?
They that, when Richard lived, would have him die,
Are now become enamour'd on his grave:
Thou, that threw'st dust upon his goodly head
When through proud London he came sighing on
After the admired heels of Bolingbroke,
Criest now 'O earth, yield us that king again,
And take thou this!' O thoughts of men accursed!
Past and to come seems best; things present worst.

Mowbray: Shall we go draw our numbers and set on?

Hastings: We are time's subjects, and time bids be gone.

Exeunt

ACT II

SCENE I

London. A street

Enter Mistress Quickly, Fang and his Boy with her, and Snare following

Mistress Quickly: Master Fang, have you entered the action?

Fang: It is entered.

Mistress Quickly: Where's your yeoman? Is't a lusty yeoman? will a' stand to 't?

Fang: Sirrah, where's Snare?

Mistress Quickly: O Lord, ay! good Master Snare.

Snare: Here, here.

Fang: Snare, we must arrest Sir John Falstaff.

Mistress Quickly: Yea, good Master Snare; I have entered him and all.

Snare: It may chance cost some of us our lives, for he will stab.

Mistress Quickly: Alas the day! take heed of him; he stabbed me in mine own house, and that most beastly: in good faith, he cares not what mischief he does. If his weapon be out: he will foin like any devil; he will spare neither man, woman, nor child.

Fang: If I can close with him, I care not for his thrust.

Mistress Quickly: No, nor I neither: I'll be at your elbow.

Fang: An I but fist him once; an a' come but within my vice,-

Mistress Quickly: I am undone by his going; I warrant you, he's an infinitive thing upon my score. Good Master Fang, hold him sure: good Master Snare, let him not 'scape. A' comes continuantly to Pie-corner- saving your manhoods- to buy a saddle; and he is indited to dinner to the Lubber's-head in Lumbert street, to Master Smooth's the silkman: I pray ye, since my exion is entered and my case so openly known to the world, let him be brought in to his answer. A hundred mark is a long one for a poor lone woman to bear: and I have borne, and borne, and borne, and have been fubbed off, and fubbed off, and fubbed off, from this day to that day, that it is a shame to be thought on. There is no honesty in such dealing; unless a woman should be made an ass and a beast, to bear every knave's wrong. Yonder he comes; and that errant malmsey-nose knave, Bardolph, with him. Do your offices, do your offices: Master Fang and Master Snare, do me, do me, do me your offices.

Enter Falstaff, Page, and Bardolph

Falstaff: How now! whose mare's dead? what's the matter?

Fang: Sir John, I arrest you at the suit of Mistress Quickly.

Falstaff: Away, varlets! Draw, Bardolph: cut me off the villain's head: throw the quean in the channel.

Mistress Quickly: Throw me in the channel! I'll throw thee in the channel. Wilt thou? wilt thou? thou bastardly rogue! Murder, murder! Ah, thou honeysuckle villain! wilt thou kill God's officers and the king's? Ah, thou honey-seed rogue! thou art a honey-seed, a man-queller, and a woman-queller.

Falstaff: Keep them off, Bardolph.

Fang: A rescue! a rescue!

Mistress Quickly: Good people, bring a rescue or two. Thou wo't, wo't thou? Thou wo't, wo't ta? do, do, thou rogue! do, thou hemp-seed!

Falstaff: Away, you scullion! you rampallion! You fustilarian! I'll tickle your catastrophe.

Enter the Lord Chief-Justice, and his men

Lord Chief-Justice: What is the matter? keep the peace here, ho!

Mistress Quickly: Good my lord, be good to me. I beseech you, stand to me.

Lord Chief-Justice: How now, Sir John! what are you brawling here?
Doth this become your place, your time and business?
You should have been well on your way to York.
Stand from him, fellow: wherefore hang'st upon him?

Mistress Quickly: O most worshipful lord, an't please your grace, I am a poor widow of Eastcheap, and he is arrested at my suit.

Lord Chief-Justice: For what sum?

Mistress Quickly: It is more than for some, my lord; it is for all, all I have. He hath eaten me out of house and home; he hath put all my substance into that fat belly of his: but I will have some of it out again, or I will ride thee o' nights like the mare.

Falstaff: I think I am as like to ride the mare, if I have any vantage of ground to get up.

Lord Chief-Justice: How comes this, Sir John? Fie! what man of good temper would endure this tempest of exclamation? Are you not ashamed to enforce a poor widow to so rough a course to come by her own?

Falstaff: What is the gross sum that I owe thee?

Mistress Quickly: Marry, if thou wert an honest man, thyself and the money too. Thou didst swear to me upon a parcel-gilt goblet, sitting in my Dolphin-chamber, at the round table, by a sea-coal fire, upon Wednesday in Wheeson week, when the prince broke thy head for liking his father to a singing-man of Windsor, thou didst swear to me then, as I was washing thy wound, to marry me and make me my lady thy wife. Canst thou deny it? Did not goodwife Keech, the butcher's wife, come in then and call me gossip Quickly? coming in to borrow a mess of vinegar; telling us she had a good dish of prawns; whereby thou didst desire to eat some; whereby I told thee they were ill for a green wound? And didst thou not, when she was gone down stairs, desire me to be no more so familiarity with such poor people; saying that ere long they should call me madam? And didst thou not kiss me and bid me fetch thee thirty shillings? I put thee now to thy book-oath: deny it, if thou canst.

Falstaff: My lord, this is a poor mad soul; and she says up and down the town that the eldest son is like you: she hath been in good case, and the truth is, poverty hath distracted her. But for these foolish officers, I beseech you I may have redress against them.

Lord Chief-Justice: Sir John, Sir John, I am well acquainted with your manner of wrenching the true cause the false way. It is not a confident brow, nor the throng of words that come with such more than impudent sauciness from you, can thrust me from a level consideration: you have, as it appears to me, practised upon the easy-yielding spirit of this woman, and made her serve your uses both in purse and in person.

Mistress Quickly: Yea, in truth, my lord.

Lord Chief-Justice: Pray thee, peace. Pay her the debt you owe her, and unpay the villany you have done her: the one you may do with sterling money, and the other with current repentance.

Falstaff: My lord, I will not undergo this sneap without reply. You call honourable boldness impudent sauciness: if a man will make courtesy and say nothing, he is virtuous: no, my lord, my humble duty remembered, I will not be your suitor. I say to you, I do desire deliverance from these officers, being upon hasty employment in the king's affairs.

Lord Chief-Justice: You speak as having power to do wrong: but answer in the effect of your reputation, and satisfy this poor woman.

Falstaff: Come hither, hostess.

Enter Gower

Lord Chief-Justice: Now, Master Gower, what news?

Gower: The king, my lord, and Harry Prince of Wales
Are near at hand: the rest the paper tells.

Falstaff: As I am a gentleman.

Mistress Quickly: Faith, you said so before.

Falstaff: As I am a gentleman. Come, no more words of it.

Mistress Quickly: By this heavenly ground I tread on, I must be fain to pawn both my plate and the tapestry of my dining-chambers.

Falstaff: Glasses, glasses is the only drinking: and for thy walls, a pretty slight drollery, or the story of the Prodigal, or the German hunting in water-work, is worth a thousand of these bed-hangings and these fly-bitten tapestries. Let it be ten pound, if thou canst. Come, an 'twere not for thy humours, there's not a better wench in England. Go, wash thy face, and draw the action. Come, thou must not be in this humour with me; dost not know me? come, come, I know thou wast set on to this.

Mistress Quickly: Pray thee, Sir John, let it be but twenty nobles: i' faith, I am loath to pawn my plate, so God save me, la!

Falstaff: Let it alone; I'll make other shift: you'll be a fool still.

Mistress Quickly: Well, you shall have it, though I pawn my gown. I hope you'll come to supper. You'll pay me all together?

Falstaff: Will I live?

To Bardolph

Go, with her, with her; hook on, hook on.

Mistress Quickly: Will you have Doll Tearsheet meet you at supper?

Falstaff: No more words; let's have her.

Exeunt Mistress Quickly, Bardolph, Officers and Boy

Lord Chief-Justice: I have heard better news.

Falstaff: What's the news, my lord?

Lord Chief-Justice: Where lay the king last night?

Gower: At Basingstoke, my lord.

Falstaff: I hope, my lord, all's well: what is the news, my lord?

Lord Chief-Justice: Come all his forces back?

Gower: No; fifteen hundred foot, five hundred horse,
Are marched up to my lord of Lancaster,
Against Northumberland and the Archbishop.

Falstaff: Comes the king back from Wales, my noble lord?

Lord Chief-Justice: You shall have letters of me presently:
Come, go along with me, good Master Gower.

Falstaff: My lord!

Lord Chief-Justice: What's the matter?

Falstaff: Master Gower, shall I entreat you with me to dinner?

Gower: I must wait upon my good lord here; I thank you, good Sir John.

Lord Chief-Justice: Sir John, you loiter here too long, being you are to take soldiers up in counties as you go.

Falstaff: Will you sup with me, Master Gower?

Lord Chief-Justice: What foolish master taught you these manners, Sir John?

Falstaff: Master Gower, if they become me not, he was a fool that taught them me. This is the right fencing grace, my lord; tap for tap, and so part fair.

Lord Chief-Justice: Now the lord lighten thee! thou art a great fool.

Exeunt

SCENE II

London. Another street

Enter Prince Henry and Poins

Prince Henry: Before God, I am exceeding weary.

Poins: Is't come to that? I had thought weariness durst not have attached one of so high blood.

Prince Henry: Faith, it does me; though it discolours the complexion of my greatness to acknowledge it. Doth it not show vilely in me to desire small beer?

Poins: Why, a prince should not be so loosely studied as to remember so weak a composition.

Prince Henry: Belike then my appetite was not princely got; for, by my troth, I do now remember the poor creature, small beer. But, indeed, these humble considerations make me out of love with my greatness. What a disgrace is it to me to remember thy name! or to know thy face to-morrow! or to take note how many pair of silk stockings thou hast, viz. these, and those that were thy peach-coloured ones! or to bear the inventory of thy shirts, as, one for superfluity, and another for use! But that the tennis-court-keeper knows better than I; for it is a low ebb of linen with thee when thou keepest not racket there; as thou hast not done a great while, because the rest of thy low countries have made a shift to eat up thy holland: and God knows, whether those that bawl out the ruins of thy linen shall inherit his kingdom: but the midwives say the children are not in the fault; whereupon the world increases, and kindreds are mightily strengthened.

Poins: How ill it follows, after you have laboured so hard, you should talk so idly! Tell me, how many good young princes would do so, their fathers being so sick as yours at this time is?

Prince Henry: Shall I tell thee one thing, Poins?

Poins: Yes, faith; and let it be an excellent good thing.

Prince Henry: It shall serve among wits of no higher breeding than thine.

Poins: Go to; I stand the push of your one thing that you will tell.

Prince Henry: Marry, I tell thee, it is not meet that I should be sad, now my father is sick: albeit I could tell thee, as to one it pleases me, for fault of a better, to call my friend, I could be sad, and sad indeed too.

Poins: Very hardly upon such a subject.

Prince Henry: By this hand thou thinkest me as far in the devil's book as thou and Falstaff for obduracy and persistency: let the end try the man. But I tell thee, my heart bleeds inwardly that my father is so sick: and keeping such vile company as thou art hath in reason taken from me all ostentation of sorrow.

Poins: The reason?

Prince Henry: What wouldst thou think of me, if I should weep?

Poins: I would think thee a most princely hypocrite.

Prince Henry: It would be every man's thought; and thou art a blessed fellow to think as every man thinks: never a man's thought in the world keeps the road-way better than thine: every man would think me an hypocrite indeed. And what accites your most worshipful thought to think so?

Poins: Why, because you have been so lewd and so much engraffed to Falstaff.

Prince Henry: And to thee.

Poins: By this light, I am well spoke on; I can hear it with my own ears: the worst that they can say of me is that I am a second brother and that I am a proper fellow of my hands; and those two things, I confess, I cannot help. By the mass, here comes Bardolph.

Enter Bardolph and Page

Prince Henry: And the boy that I gave Falstaff: a' had him from me Christian; and look, if the fat villain have not transformed him ape.

Bardolph: God save your grace!

Prince Henry: And yours, most noble Bardolph!

Bardolph: Come, you virtuous ass, you bashful fool, must you be blushing? wherefore blush you now? What a maidenly man-at-arms are you become! Is't such a matter to get a pottle-pot's maidenhead?

Page: A' calls me e'en now, my lord, through a red lattice, and I could discern no part of his face from the window: at last I spied his eyes, and methought he had made two holes in the ale-wife's new petticoat and so peeped through.

Prince Henry: Has not the boy profited?

Bardolph: Away, you whoreson upright rabbit, away!

Page: Away, you rascally Althaea's dream, away!

Prince Henry: Instruct us, boy; what dream, boy?

Page: Marry, my lord, Althaea dreamed she was delivered of a fire-brand; and therefore I call him her dream.

Prince Henry: A crown's worth of good interpretation: there 'tis, boy.

Poins: O, that this good blossom could be kept from cankers! Well, there is sixpence to preserve thee.

Bardolph: An you do not make him hanged among you, the gallows shall have wrong.

Prince Henry: And how doth thy master, Bardolph?

Bardolph: Well, my lord. He heard of your grace's coming to town: there's a letter for you.

Poins: Delivered with good respect. And how doth the martlemas, your master?

Bardolph: In bodily health, sir.

Poins: Marry, the immortal part needs a physician; but that moves not him: though that be sick, it dies not.

Prince Henry: I do allow this wen to be as familiar with me as my dog; and he holds his place; for look you how he writes.

Poins *[Reads]*: 'John Falstaff, knight,'- every man must know that, as oft as he has occasion to name himself: even like those that are kin to the king; for they never prick their finger but they say, 'There's some of the king's blood spilt.' 'How comes that?' says he, that takes upon him not to conceive. The answer is as ready as a borrower's cap, 'I am the king's poor cousin, sir.'

Prince Henry: Nay, they will be kin to us, or they will fetch it from Japhet. But to the letter.

Poins *[Reads]:* 'Sir John Falstaff, knight, to the son of the king, nearest his father, Harry Prince of Wales, greeting.' Why, this is a certificate.

Prince Henry: Peace!

Poins *[Reads]:* 'I will imitate the honourable Romans in brevity:' he sure means brevity in breath, short-winded. 'I commend me to thee, I commend thee, and I leave thee. Be not too familiar with Poins; for he misuses thy favours so much, that he swears thou art to marry his sister Nell. Repent at idle times as thou mayest; and so, farewell. Thine, by yea and no, which is as much as to say, as thou usest him, Jack Falstaff with my familiars, John with my brothers and sisters, and Sir John with all Europe.'

My lord, I'll steep this letter in sack and make him eat it.

Prince Henry: That's to make him eat twenty of his words. But do you use me thus, Ned? must I marry your sister?

Poins: God send the wench no worse fortune! But I never said so.

Prince Henry: Well, thus we play the fools with the time, and the spirits of the wise sit in the clouds and mock us. Is your master here in London?

Bardolph: Yea, my lord.

Prince Henry: Where sups he? doth the old boar feed in the old frank?

Bardolph: At the old place, my lord, in Eastcheap.

Prince Henry: What company?

Page: Ephesians, my lord, of the old church.

Prince Henry: Sup any women with him?

Page: None, my lord, but old Mistress Quickly and Mistress Doll Tearsheet.

Prince Henry: What pagan may that be?

Page: A proper gentlewoman, sir, and a kinswoman of my master's.

Prince Henry: Even such kin as the parish heifers are to the town bull. Shall we steal upon them, Ned, at supper?

Poins: I am your shadow, my lord; I'll follow you.

Prince Henry: Sirrah, you boy, and Bardolph, no word to your master that I am yet come to town: there's for your silence.

Bardolph: I have no tongue, sir.

Page: And for mine, sir, I will govern it.

Prince Henry: Fare you well; go.

Exeunt Bardolph and Page

This Doll Tearsheet should be some road.

Poins: I warrant you, as common as the way between Saint Alban's and London.

Prince Henry: How might we see Falstaff bestow himself to-night in his true colours, and not ourselves be seen?

Poins: Put on two leathern jerkins and aprons, and wait upon him at his table as drawers.

Prince Henry: From a God to a bull? a heavy descension! it was Jove's case. From a prince to a prentice? a low transformation! that shall be mine; for in every thing the purpose must weigh with the folly. Follow me, Ned.

Exeunt

SCENE III

Warkworth. Before the castle

Enter Northumberland, Lady Northumberland, and Lady Percy

Northumberland: I pray thee, loving wife, and gentle daughter,
Give even way unto my rough affairs:
Put not you on the visage of the times
And be like them to Percy troublesome.

Lady Northumberland: I have given over, I will speak no more:
Do what you will; your wisdom be your guide.

Northumberland: Alas, sweet wife, my honour is at pawn;
And, but my going, nothing can redeem it.

Lady Percy: O yet, for God's sake, go not to these wars!
The time was, father, that you broke your word,
When you were more endeared to it than now;
When your own Percy, when my heart's dear Harry,
Threw many a northward look to see his father
Bring up his powers; but he did long in vain.
Who then persuaded you to stay at home?
There were two honours lost, yours and your son's.
For yours, the God of heaven brighten it!
For his, it stuck upon him as the sun
In the grey vault of heaven, and by his light
Did all the chivalry of England move
To do brave acts: he was indeed the glass
Wherein the noble youth did dress themselves:
He had no legs that practised not his gait;
And speaking thick, which nature made his blemish,
Became the accents of the valiant;

For those that could speak low and tardily
Would turn their own perfection to abuse,
To seem like him: so that in speech, in gait,
In diet, in affections of delight,
In military rules, humours of blood,
He was the mark and glass, copy and book,
That fashion'd others. And him, O wondrous him!
O miracle of men! him did you leave,
Second to none, unseconded by you,
To look upon the hideous god of war
In disadvantage; to abide a field
Where nothing but the sound of Hotspur's name
Did seem defensible: so you left him.
Never, O never, do his ghost the wrong
To hold your honour more precise and nice
With others than with him! let them alone:
The marshal and the archbishop are strong:
Had my sweet Harry had but half their numbers,
To-day might I, hanging on Hotspur's neck,
Have talk'd of Monmouth's grave.

Northumberland: Beshrew your heart,
Fair daughter, you do draw my spirits from me
With new lamenting ancient oversights.
But I must go and meet with danger there,
Or it will seek me in another place
And find me worse provided.

Lady Northumberland: O, fly to Scotland,
Till that the nobles and the armed commons
Have of their puissance made a little taste.

Lady Percy: If they get ground and vantage of the king,
Then join you with them, like a rib of steel,
To make strength stronger; but, for all our loves,
First let them try themselves. So did your son;
He was so suffer'd: so came I a widow;
And never shall have length of life enough
To rain upon remembrance with mine eyes,
That it may grow and sprout as high as heaven,
For recordation to my noble husband.

Northumberland: Come, come, go in with me. 'Tis with my mind
As with the tide swell'd up unto his height,
That makes a still-stand, running neither way:
Fain would I go to meet the archbishop,
But many thousand reasons hold me back.
I will resolve for Scotland: there am I,
Till time and vantage crave my company.

Exeunt

SCENE IV

London. The Boar's-head Tavern in Eastcheap

Enter two Drawers

First Drawer: What the devil hast thou brought there? apple-johns? thou knowest Sir John cannot endure an apple-john.

Second Drawer: Mass, thou sayest true. The prince once set a dish of apple-johns before him, and told him there were five more Sir Johns, and, putting off his hat, said 'I will now take my leave of these six dry, round, old, withered knights.' It angered him to the heart: but he hath forgot that.

First Drawer: Why, then, cover, and set them down: and see if thou canst find out Sneak's noise; Mistress Tearsheet would fain hear some music. Dispatch: the room where they supped is too hot; they'll come in straight.

Second Drawer: Sirrah, here will be the prince and Master Poins: anon; and they will put on two of our jerkins and aprons; and Sir John must not know of it: Bardolph hath brought word.

First Drawer: By the mass, here will be old Utis: it will be an excellent stratagem.

Second Drawer: I'll see if I can find out Sneak.

Exit

Enter Mistress Quickly and Doll Tearsheet

Mistress Quickly: I' faith, sweetheart, methinks now you are in an excellent good temperality: your pulsidge beats as extraordinarily as heart would desire; and your colour, I warrant you, is as red as any rose, in good truth, la! But, i' faith, you have drunk too much canaries; and that's a marvellous searching wine, and it perfumes the blood ere one can say 'What's this?' How do you now?

Doll Tearsheet: Better than I was: hem!

Mistress Quickly: Why, that's well said; a good heart's worth gold. Lo, here comes Sir John.

Enter Falstaff

Falstaff *[Singing]*: 'When Arthur first in court,'
- Empty the jordan.

Exit First Drawer

Singing

- 'nd was a worthy king.' How now, Mistress Doll!

Mistress Quickly: Sick of a calm; yea, good faith.

Falstaff: So is all her sect; an they be once in a calm, they are sick.

Doll Tearsheet: You muddy rascal, is that all the comfort you give me?

Falstaff: You make fat rascals, Mistress Doll.

Doll Tearsheet: I make them! gluttony and diseases make them; I make them not.

Falstaff: If the cook help to make the gluttony, you help to make the diseases, Doll: we catch of you, Doll, we catch of you; grant that, my poor virtue grant that.

Doll Tearsheet: Yea, joy, our chains and our jewels.

Falstaff: 'Your broaches, pearls, and ouches:' for to serve bravely is to come halting off, you know: to come off the breach with his pike bent bravely, and to surgery bravely; to venture upon the charged chambers bravely,-

Doll Tearsheet: Hang yourself, you muddy conger, hang yourself!

Mistress Quickly: By my troth, this is the old fashion; you two never meet but you fall to some discord: you are both, i' good truth, as rheumatic as two dry toasts; you cannot one bear with another's confirmities. What the good-year! one must bear, and that must be you: you are the weaker vessel, as they say, the emptier vessel.

Doll Tearsheet: Can a weak empty vessel bear such a huge full hogshead? there's a whole merchant's venture of Bourdeaux stuff in him; you have not seen a hulk better stuffed in the hold. Come, I'll be friends with thee, Jack: thou art going to the wars; and whether I shall ever see thee again or no, there is nobody cares.

Re-enter First Drawer

First Drawer: Sir, Ancient Pistol's below, and would speak with you.

Doll Tearsheet: Hang him, swaggering rascal! let him not come hither: it is the foul-mouthed'st rogue in England.

Mistress Quickly: If he swagger, let him not come here: no, by my faith; I must live among my neighbours: I'll no swaggerers: I am in good name and fame with the very best: shut the door; there comes no swaggerers here: I have not lived all this while, to have swaggering now: shut the door, I pray you.

Falstaff: Dost thou hear, hostess?

Mistress Quickly: Pray ye, pacify yourself, Sir John: there comes no swaggerers here.

Falstaff: Dost thou hear? it is mine ancient.

Mistress Quickly: Tilly-fally, Sir John, ne'er tell me: your ancient swaggerer comes not in my doors. I was before Master Tisick, the debuty, t'other day; and, as he said to me, 'twas no longer ago than Wednesday last, 'I' good faith, neighbour Quickly,' says he; Master Dumbe, our minister, was by then; 'neighbour Quickly,' says he, 'receive those that are civil; for,' said he, 'you are in an ill name:' now a' said so, I can tell whereupon; 'for,' says he, 'you are an honest woman, and well thought on; therefore take heed what guests you receive: receive,' says he, 'no swaggering companions.' There comes none here: you would bless you to hear what he said: no, I'll no swaggerers.

Falstaff: He's no swaggerer, hostess; a tame cheater, i' faith; you may stroke him as gently as a puppy greyhound: he'll not swagger with a Barbary hen, if her feathers turn back in any show of resistance. Call him up, drawer.

Exit First Drawer

Mistress Quickly: Cheater, call you him? I will bar no honest man my house, nor no cheater: but I do not love swaggering, by my troth; I am the worse, when one says swagger: feel, masters, how I shake; look you, I warrant you.

Doll Tearsheet: So you do, hostess.

Mistress Quickly: Do I? yea, in very truth, do I, an 'twere an aspen leaf: I cannot abide swaggerers.

Enter Pistol, Bardolph, and Page

Pistol: God save you, Sir John!

Falstaff: Welcome, Ancient Pistol. Here, Pistol, I charge you with a cup of sack: do you discharge upon mine hostess.

Pistol: I will discharge upon her, Sir John, with two bullets.

Falstaff: She is Pistol-proof, sir; you shall hardly offend her.

Mistress Quickly: Come, I'll drink no proofs nor no bullets: I'll drink no more than will do me good, for no man's pleasure, I.

Pistol: Then to you, Mistress Dorothy; I will charge you.

Doll Tearsheet: Charge me! I scorn you, scurvy companion. What! you poor, base, rascally, cheating, lack-linen mate! Away, you Mouldy rogue, away! I am meat for your master.

Pistol: I know you, Mistress Dorothy.

Doll Tearsheet: Away, you cut-purse rascal! you filthy bung, away! by this wine, I'll thrust my knife in your Mouldy chaps, an you play the saucy cuttle with me. Away, you bottle-ale rascal! you basket-hilt stale juggler, you! Since when, I pray you, sir? God's light, with two points on your shoulder? much!

Pistol: God let me not live, but I will murder your ruff for this.

Falstaff: No more, Pistol; I would not have you go off here: discharge yourself of our company, Pistol.

Mistress Quickly: No, Good Captain Pistol; not here, sweet captain.

Doll Tearsheet: Captain! thou abominable damned cheater, art thou not ashamed to be called captain? An captains were of my mind, they would truncheon you out, for taking their names upon you before you have earned them. You a captain! you slave, for what? for tearing a poor whore's ruff in a bawdy-house? He a captain! hang him, rogue! he lives upon Mouldy stewed prunes and dried cakes. A captain! God's light, these villains will make the word as odious as the word 'occupy;' which was an excellent good word before it was ill sorted: therefore captains had need look to 't.

Bardolph: Pray thee, go down, good ancient.

Falstaff: Hark thee hither, Mistress Doll.

Pistol: Not I: I tell thee what, Corporal Bardolph, I could tear her: I'll be revenged of her.

Page: Pray thee, go down.

Pistol: I'll see her damned first; to Pluto's damned lake, by this hand, to the infernal deep, with Erebus and tortures vile also. Hold hook and line, say I. Down, down, dogs! down, faitors! Have we not Hiren here?

Mistress Quickly: Good Captain Peesel, be quiet; 'tis very late, i' faith: I beseek you now, aggravate your choler.

Pistol: These be good humours, indeed! Shall pack-horses
And hollow pamper'd jades of Asia,
Which cannot go but thirty mile a-day,
Compare with Caesars, and with Cannibals,
And Trojan Greeks? nay, rather damn them with
King Cerberus; and let the welkin roar.
Shall we fall foul for toys?

Mistress Quickly: By my troth, captain, these are very bitter words.

Bardolph: Be gone, good ancient: this will grow to abrawl anon.

Pistol: Die men like dogs! give crowns like pins! Have we not Heren here?

Mistress Quickly: O' my word, captain, there's none such here. What the good-year! do you think I would deny her? For God's sake, be quiet.

Pistol: Then feed, and be fat, my fair Calipolis.
Come, give's some sack.
'Si fortune me tormente, sperato me contento.'
Fear we broadsides? no, let the fiend give fire:
Give me some sack: and, sweetheart, lie thou there.

Laying down his sword

Come we to full points here; and are etceteras nothing?

Falstaff: Pistol, I would be quiet.

Pistol: Sweet knight, I kiss thy neaf: what! we have seen the seven stars.

Doll Tearsheet: For God's sake, thrust him down stairs: I cannot endure such a fustian rascal.

Pistol: Thrust him down stairs! know we not Galloway nags?

Falstaff: Quoit him down, Bardolph, like a shove-groat shilling: nay, an a' do nothing but speak nothing, a' shall be nothing here.

Bardolph: Come, get you down stairs.

Pistol: What! shall we have incision? shall we imbrue?

Snatching up his sword

Then death rock me asleep, abridge my doleful days!
Why, then, let grievous, ghastly, gaping wounds
Untwine the Sisters Three! Come, Atropos, I say!

Mistress Quickly: Here's goodly stuff toward!

Falstaff: Give me my rapier, boy.

Doll Tearsheet: I pray thee, Jack, I pray thee, do not draw.

Falstaff: Get you down stairs.

Drawing, and driving Pistol out

Mistress Quickly: Here's a goodly tumult! I'll forswear keeping house, afore I'll be in these tirrits and frights. So; murder, I warrant now. Alas, alas! put up your naked weapons, put up your naked weapons.

Exeunt Pistol and Bardolph

Doll Tearsheet: I pray thee, Jack, be quiet; the rascal's gone. Ah, you whoreson little valiant villain, you!

Mistress Quickly: He you not hurt i' the groin? methought a' made a shrewd thrust at your belly.

Re-enter Bardolph

Falstaff: Have you turned him out o' doors?

Bardolph: Yea, sir. The rascal's drunk: you have hurt him, sir, i' the shoulder.

Falstaff: A rascal! to brave me!

Doll Tearsheet: Ah, you sweet little rogue, you! alas, poor ape, how thou sweatest! come, let me wipe thy face; come on, you whoreson chops: ah, rogue! i'faith, I love thee: thou art as valorous as Hector of Troy, worth five of Agamemnon, and ten times better than the Nine Worthies: ah, villain!

Falstaff: A rascally slave! I will toss the rogue in a blanket.

Doll Tearsheet: Do, an thou darest for thy heart: an thou dost, I'll canvass thee between a pair of sheets.

Enter Music

Page: The music is come, sir.

Falstaff: Let them play. Play, sirs. Sit on my knee, Doll. A rascal bragging slave! the rogue fled from me like quicksilver.

Doll Tearsheet: I' faith, and thou followedst him like a church. Thou whoreson little tidy Bartholomew boar-pig, when wilt thou leave fighting o' days and foining o' nights, and begin to patch up thine old body for heaven?

Enter, behind, Prince Henry and Poins, disguised

Falstaff: Peace, good Doll! do not speak like a death's-head; do not bid me remember mine end.

Doll Tearsheet: Sirrah, what humour's the prince of?

Falstaff: A good shallow young fellow: a' would have made a good pantler, a' would ha' chipp'd bread well.

Doll Tearsheet: They say Poins has a good wit.

Falstaff: He a good wit? hang him, baboon! his wit's as thick as Tewksbury mustard; there's no more conceit in him than is in a mallet.

Doll Tearsheet: Why does the prince love him so, then?

Falstaff: Because their legs are both of a bigness, and a' plays at quoits well, and eats conger and fennel, and drinks off candles' ends for flap-dragons, and rides the wild-mare with the boys, and jumps upon joined-stools, and swears with a good grace, and wears his boots very smooth, like unto the sign of the leg, and breeds no bate with telling of discreet stories; and such other gambol faculties a' has, that show a weak mind and an able body, for the which the prince admits him: for the prince himself is such another; the weight of a hair will turn the scales between their avoirdupois.

Prince Henry: Would not this nave of a wheel have his ears cut off?

Poins: Let's beat him before his whore.

Prince Henry: Look, whether the withered elder hath not his poll clawed like a parrot.

Poins: Is it not strange that desire should so many years outlive performance?

Falstaff: Kiss me, Doll.

Prince Henry: Saturn and Venus this year in conjunction! what says the almanac to that?

Poins: And look, whether the fiery Trigon, his man, be not lisping to his master's old tables, his note-book, his counsel-keeper.

Falstaff: Thou dost give me flattering busses.

Doll Tearsheet: By my troth, I kiss thee with a most constant heart.

Falstaff: I am old, I am old.

Doll Tearsheet: I love thee better than I love e'er a scurvy young boy of them all.

Falstaff: What stuff wilt have a kirtle of? I shall receive money o' Thursday: shalt have a cap to-morrow. A merry song, come: it grows late; we'll to bed. Thou'lt forget me when I am gone.

Doll Tearsheet: By my troth, thou'lt set me a-weeping, an thou sayest so: prove that ever I dress myself handsome till thy return: well, harken at the end.

Falstaff: Some sack, Francis.

Prince Henry Poins: Anon, anon, sir.

Coming forward

Falstaff: Ha! a bastard son of the king's? And art not thou Poins his brother?

Prince Henry: Why, thou globe of sinful continents! what a life dost thou lead!

Falstaff: A better than thou: I am a gentleman; thou art a drawer.

Prince Henry: Very true, sir; and I come to draw you out by the ears.

Mistress Quickly: O, the Lord preserve thy good grace! by my troth, welcome to London. Now, the Lord bless that sweet face of thine! O, Jesu, are you come from Wales?

Falstaff: Thou whoreson mad compound of majesty, by this light flesh and corrupt blood, thou art welcome.

Doll Tearsheet: How, you fat fool! I scorn you.

Poins: My lord, he will drive you out of your revenge and turn all to a merriment, if you take not the heat.

Prince Henry: You whoreson candle-mine, you, how vilely did you speak of me even now before this honest, virtuous, civil gentlewoman!

Mistress Quickly: God's blessing of your good heart! and so she is, by my troth.

Falstaff: Didst thou hear me?

Prince Henry: Yea, and you knew me, as you did when you ran away by Gad's-hill: you knew I was at your back, and spoke it on purpose to try my patience.

Falstaff: No, no, no; not so; I did not think thou wast within hearing.

Prince Henry: I shall drive you then to confess the wilful abuse; and then I know how to handle you.

Falstaff: No abuse, Hal, o' mine honour, no abuse.

Prince Henry: Not to dispraise me, and call me pantier and bread-chipper and I know not what?

Falstaff: No abuse, Hal.

Poins: No abuse?

Falstaff: No abuse, Ned, i' the world; honest Ned, none. I dispraised him before the wicked, that the wicked might not fall in love with him; in which doing, I have done the part of a careful friend and a true subject, and thy father is to give me thanks for it. No abuse, Hal: none, Ned, none: no, faith, boys, none.

Prince Henry: See now, whether pure fear and entire cowardice doth not make thee wrong this virtuous gentlewoman to close with us? is she of the wicked? is thine hostess here of the wicked? or is thy boy of the wicked? or honest Bardolph, whose zeal burns in his nose, of the wicked?

Poins: Answer, thou dead elm, answer.

Falstaff: The fiend hath pricked down Bardolph irrecoverable; and his face is Lucifer's privy-kitchen, where he doth nothing but roast malt-worms. For the boy, there is a good angel about him; but the devil outbids him too.

Prince Henry: For the women?

Falstaff: For one of them, she is in hell already, and burns poor souls. For the other, I owe her money, and whether she be damned for that, I know not.

Mistress Quickly: No, I warrant you.

Falstaff: No, I think thou art not; I think thou art quit for that. Marry, there is another indictment upon thee, for suffering flesh to be eaten in thy house, contrary to the law; for the which I think thou wilt howl.

Mistress Quickly: All victuallers do so; what's a joint of mutton or two in a whole Lent?

Prince Henry: You, gentlewoman,-

Doll Tearsheet: What says your grace?

Falstaff: His grace says that which his flesh rebels against.

Knocking within

Mistress Quickly: Who knocks so loud at door? Look to the door there, Francis.

Enter Peto

Prince Henry: Peto, how now! what news?

Peto: The king your father is at Westminster:
And there are twenty weak and wearied posts
Come from the north: and, as I came along,
I met and overtook a dozen captains,
Bare-headed, sweating, knocking at the taverns,
And asking everyone for Sir John Falstaff.

Prince Henry: By heaven, Poins, I feel me much to blame,
So idly to profane the precious time,
When tempest of commotion, like the south
Borne with black vapour, doth begin to melt
And drop upon our bare unarmed heads.
Give me my sword and cloak. Falstaff, good night.

Exeunt Prince Henry, Poins, Peto and Bardolph

Falstaff: Now comes in the sweetest morsel of the night, and we must hence and leave it unpicked.

Knocking within

More knocking at the door!

Re-enter Bardolph

How now! what's the matter?

Bardolph: You must away to court, sir, presently;
A dozen captains stay at door for you.

Falstaff *[To the Page]* Pay the musicians, sirrah. Farewell, hostess; farewell, Doll. You see, my good wenches, how men of merit are sought after: the undeserver may sleep, when the man of action is called on. Farewell good wenches: if I be not sent away post, I will see you again ere I go.

Doll Tearsheet: I cannot speak; if my heart be not read to burst,- well, sweet Jack, have a care of thyself.

Falstaff: Farewell, farewell.

Exeunt Falstaff and Bardolph

Mistress Quickly: Well, fare thee well: I have known thee these twenty-nine years, come peascod-time; but an honester and truer-hearted man,- well, fare thee well.

Bardolph *[Within]:* Mistress Tearsheet!

Mistress Quickly: What's the matter?

Bardolph *[Within]:* Good Mistress Tearsheet, come to my master.

Mistress Quickly: O, run, Doll, run; run, good Doll: come.

She comes blubbered

Yea, will you come, Doll?

Exeunt

ACT III

SCENE I

Westminster. The palace

Enter King Henry IV in his nightgown, with a Page

King Henry IV: Go call the Earls of Surrey and of Warwick;
But, ere they come, bid them o'er-read these letters,
And well consider of them; make good speed.

Exit Page

How many thousand of my poorest subjects
Are at this hour asleep! O sleep, O gentle sleep,
Nature's soft nurse, how have I frighted thee,
That thou no more wilt weigh my eyelids down
And steep my senses in forgetfulness?
Why rather, sleep, liest thou in smoky cribs,
Upon uneasy pallets stretching thee
And hush'd with buzzing night-flies to thy slumber,
Than in the perfumed chambers of the great,
Under the canopies of costly state,
And lull'd with sound of sweetest melody?
O thou dull god, why liest thou with the vile
In loathsome beds, and leavest the kingly couch
A watch-case or a common 'larum-bell?
Wilt thou upon the high and giddy mast
Seal up the ship-boy's eyes, and rock his brains
In cradle of the rude imperious surge
And in the visitation of the winds,
Who take the ruffian billows by the top,
Curling their monstrous heads and hanging them

With deafening clamour in the slippery clouds,
That, with the hurly, death itself awakes?
Canst thou, O partial sleep, give thy repose
To the wet sea-boy in an hour so rude,
And in the calmest and most stillest night,
With all appliances and means to boot,
Deny it to a king? Then happy low, lie down!
Uneasy lies the head that wears a crown.

Enter Warwick and Surrey

Warwick: Many good morrows to your majesty!
King Henry IV: Is it good morrow, lords?
Warwick: 'Tis one o'clock, and past.
King Henry IV: Why, then, good morrow to you all, my lords.
Have you read o'er the letters that I sent you?
Warwick: We have, my liege.
King Henry IV: Then you perceive the body of our kingdom
How foul it is; what rank diseases grow
And with what danger, near the heart of it.
Warwick: It is but as a body yet distemper'd;
Which to his former strength may be restored
With good advice and little medicine:
My Lord Northumberland will soon be cool'd.
King Henry IV: O God! that one might read the book of fate,
And see the revolution of the times
Make mountains level, and the continent,
Weary of solid firmness, melt itself
Into the sea! and, other times, to see
The beachy girdle of the ocean
Too wide for Neptune's hips; how chances mock,

And changes fill the cup of alteration
With divers liquors! O, if this were seen,
The happiest youth, viewing his progress through,
What perils past, what crosses to ensue,
Would shut the book, and sit him down and die.
'Tis not 'ten years gone
Since Richard and Northumberland, great friends,
Did feast together, and in two years after
Were they at wars: it is but eight years since
This Percy was the man nearest my soul,
Who like a brother toil'd in my affairs
And laid his love and life under my foot,
Yea, for my sake, even to the eyes of Richard
Gave him defiance. But which of you was by-
You, cousin Nevil, as I may remember-
To Warwick
When Richard, with his eye brimful of tears,
Then cheque'd and rated by Northumberland,
Did speak these words, now proved a prophecy?
'Northumberland, thou ladder by the which
My cousin Bolingbroke ascends my throne;'
Though then, God knows, I had no such intent,
But that necessity so bow'd the state
That I and greatness were compell'd to kiss:
'The time shall come,' thus did he follow it,
'The time will come, that foul sin, gathering head,
Shall break into corruption:' so went on,
Foretelling this same time's condition
And the division of our amity.

Warwick: There is a history in all men's lives,
Figuring the nature of the times deceased;

The which observed, a man may prophesy,
With a near aim, of the main chance of things
As yet not come to life, which in their seeds
And weak beginnings lie intreasured.
Such things become the hatch and brood of time;
And by the necessary form of this
King Richard might create a perfect guess
That great Northumberland, then false to him,
Would of that seed grow to a greater falseness;
Which should not find a ground to root upon,
Unless on you.

King Henry IV: Are these things then necessities?
Then let us meet them like necessities:
And that same word even now cries out on us:
They say the bishop and Northumberland: Are fifty thousand strong.

Warwick: It cannot be, my lord;
Rumour doth double, like the voice and echo,
The numbers of the fear'd. Please it your grace
To go to bed. Upon my soul, my lord,
The powers that you already have sent forth
Shall bring this prize in very easily.
To comfort you the more, I have received
A certain instance that Glendower is dead.
Your majesty hath been this fortnight ill,
And these unseason'd hours perforce must add
Unto your sickness.

King Henry IV: I will take your counsel:
And were these inward wars once out of hand,
We would, dear lords, unto the Holy Land.

Exeunt

SCENE II

Gloucestershire. Before Shallow's house

Enter Shallow and Silence, meeting; Mouldy, Shadow, Wart, Feeble, Bullcalf, a Servant or two with them

Shallow: Come on, come on, come on, sir; give me your hand, sir, give me your hand, sir: an early stirrer, by the rood! And how doth my good cousin Silence?

Silence: Good morrow, good cousin Shallow.

Shallow: And how doth my cousin, your bedfellow? and your fairest daughter and mine, my god-daughter Ellen?

Silence: Alas, a black ousel, cousin Shallow!

Shallow: By yea and nay, sir, I dare say my cousin William is become a good scholar: he is at Oxford still, is he not?

Silence: Indeed, sir, to my cost.

Shallow: A' must, then, to the inns o' court shortly. I was once of Clement's Inn, where I think they will talk of mad Shallow yet.

Silence: You were called 'lusty Shallow' then, cousin.

Shallow: By the mass, I was called anything; and I would have done anything indeed too, and roundly too. There was I, and little John Doit of Staffordshire, and black George Barnes, and Francis Pickbone, and Will Squele, a Cotswold man; you had not four such swinge-bucklers in all the inns o' court again: and I may say to you, we knew where the bona-robas were and had the best of them all at commandment. Then was Jack Falstaff, now Sir John, a boy, and page to Thomas Mowbray, Duke of Norfolk.

Silence: This Sir John, cousin, that comes hither anon about soldiers?

Shallow: The same Sir John, the very same. I see him break Skogan's head at the court-gate, when a' was a crack not thus high: and the very same day did I fight with one Sampson Stockfish, a fruiterer, behind Gray's Inn. Jesu, Jesu, the mad days that I have spent! and to see how many of my old acquaintance are dead!

Silence: We shall all follow, cousin.

Shadow: Certain, 'tis certain; very sure, very sure: death, as the Psalmist saith, is certain to all; all shall die. How a good yoke of bullocks at Stamford fair?

Silence: By my troth, I was not there.

Shallow: Death is certain. Is old Double of your town living yet?

Silence: Dead, sir.

Shallow: Jesu, Jesu, dead! a' drew a good bow; and dead! a' shot a fine shoot: John a Gaunt loved him well, and betted much money on his head. Dead! a' would have clapped i' the clout at twelve score; and carried you a forehand shaft a fourteen and fourteen and a half, that it would have done a man's heart good to see. How a score of ewes now?

Silence: Thereafter as they be: a score of good ewes may be worth ten pounds.

Shallow: And is old Double dead?

Silence: Here come two of Sir John Falstaff's men, as I think.

Enter Bardolph and one with him

Bardolph: Good morrow, honest gentlemen: I beseech you, which is Justice Shallow?

Shallow: I am Robert Shallow, sir; a poor esquire of this county, and one of the king's justices of the peace: What is your good pleasure with me?

Bardolph: My captain, sir, commends him to you; my captain, Sir John Falstaff, a tall gentleman, by heaven, and a most gallant leader.

Shallow: He greets me well, sir. I knew him a good backsword man. How doth the good knight? may I ask how my lady his wife doth?

Bardolph: Sir, pardon; a soldier is better accommodated than with a wife.

Shallow: It is well said, in faith, sir; and it is well said indeed too. Better accommodated! it is good; yea, indeed, is it: good phrases are surely, and ever were, very commendable. Accommodated! it comes of 'accommodo' very good; a good phrase.

Bardolph: Pardon me, sir; I have heard the word. Phrase call you it? by this good day, I know not the phrase; but I will maintain the word with my sword to be a soldier-like word, and a word of exceeding good command, by heaven. Accommodated; that is, when a man is, as they say, accommodated; or when a man is, being, whereby a' may be thought to be accommodated; which is an excellent thing.

Shallow: It is very just.

Enter Falstaff

Look, here comes good Sir John. Give me your good hand, give me your worship's good hand: by my troth, you like well and bear your years very well: welcome, good Sir John.

Falstaff: I am glad to see you well, good Master Robert.

Shallow: Master Surecard, as I think?

Shallow: No, Sir John; it is my cousin Silence, in commission with me.

Falstaff: Good Master Silence, it well befits you should be of the peace.

Silence: Your good-worship is welcome.

Falstaff: Fie! this is hot weather, gentlemen. Have you provided me here half a dozen sufficient men?

Shallow: Marry, have we, sir. Will you sit?

Falstaff: Let me see them, I beseech you.

Shallow: Where's the roll? where's the roll? where's the roll? Let me see, let me see, let me see. So, so: yea, marry, sir: Ralph Mouldy! Let them appear as I call; let them do so, let them do so. Let me see; where is Mouldy?

Mouldy: Here, an't please you.

Shallow: What think you, Sir John? a good-limbed fellow; young, strong, and of good friends.

Falstaff: Is thy name Mouldy?

Mouldy: Yea, an't please you.

Falstaff: 'Tis the more time thou wert used.

Shallow: Ha, ha, ha! most excellent, i' faith! Things that are Mouldy lack use: very singular good! in faith, well said, Sir John, very well said.

Falstaff: Prick him.

Mouldy: I was pricked well enough before, an you could have let me alone: my old dame will be undone now for one to do her husbandry and her drudgery: you need not to have pricked me; there are other men fitter to go out than I.

Falstaff: Go to: peace, Mouldy; you shall go. Mouldy, it is time you were spent.

Mouldy: Spent!

Shallow: Peace, fellow, peace; stand aside: know you where you are? For the other, Sir John: let me see: Simon Shadow!

Falstaff: Yea, marry, let me have him to sit under: he's like to be a cold soldier.

Shallow: Where's Shadow?

Shadow: Here, sir.

Falstaff: Shadow, whose son art thou?

Shadow: My mother's son, sir.

Falstaff: Thy mother's son! like enough, and thy father's shadow: so the son of the female is the shadow of the male: it is often so, indeed; but much of the father's substance!

Shallow: Do you like him, Sir John?

Falstaff: Shadow will serve for summer; prick him, for we have a number of shadows to fill up the muster-book.

Shallow: Thomas Wart!

Falstaff: Where's he?

Wart: Here, sir.

Falstaff: Is thy name Wart?

Wart: Yea, sir.

Falstaff: Thou art a very ragged Wart.

Shallow: Shall I prick him down, Sir John?

Falstaff: It were superfluous; for his apparel is built upon his back and the whole frame stands upon pins: prick him no more.

Shallow: Ha, ha, ha! you can do it, sir; you can do it: I commend you well. Francis Feeble!

Feeble: Here, sir.

Falstaff: What trade art thou, Feeble?

Feeble: A woman's tailor, sir.

Shallow: Shall I prick him, sir?

Falstaff: You may: but if he had been a man's tailor, he'ld ha' pricked you. Wilt thou make as many holes in an enemy's battle as thou hast done in a woman's petticoat?

Feeble: I will do my good will, sir; you can have no more.

Falstaff: Well said, good woman's tailor! well said, courageous Feeble! thou wilt be as valiant as the wrathful dove or most magnanimous mouse. Prick the woman's tailor: well, Master Shallow; deep, Master Shallow.

Feeble: I would Wart might have gone, sir.

Falstaff: I would thou wert a man's tailor, that thou mightst mend him and make him fit to go. I cannot put him to a private soldier that is the leader of so many thousands: let that suffice, most forcible Feeble.

Feeble: It shall suffice, sir.

Falstaff: I am bound to thee, reverend Feeble. Who is next?

Shallow: Peter Bullcalf o' the green!

Falstaff: Yea, marry, let's see Bullcalf.

Bullcalf: Here, sir.

Falstaff: 'Fore God, a likely fellow! Come, prick me Bullcalf till he roar again.

Bullcalf: O Lord! good my lord captain,-

Falstaff: What, dost thou roar before thou art pricked?

Bullcalf: O Lord, sir! I am a diseased man.

Falstaff: What disease hast thou?

Bullcalf: A whoreson cold, sir, a cough, sir, which I caught with ringing in the king's affairs upon his coronation-day, sir.

Falstaff: Come, thou shalt go to the wars in a gown; we wilt have away thy cold; and I will take such order that my friends shall ring for thee. Is here all?

Shallow: Here is two more called than your number, you must have but four here, sir: and so, I pray you, go in with me to dinner.

Falstaff: Come, I will go drink with you, but I cannot tarry dinner. I am glad to see you, by my troth, Master Shallow.

Shallow: O, Sir John, do you remember since we lay all night in the windmill in Saint George's field?

Falstaff: No more of that, good Master Shallow, no more of that.

Shallow: Ha! 'twas a merry night. And is Jane Nightwork alive?

Falstaff: She lives, Master Shallow.

Shallow: She never could away with me.

Falstaff: Never, never; she would always say she could not abide Master Shallow.

Shallow: By the mass, I could anger her to the heart. She was then a bona-roba. Doth she hold her own well?

Falstaff: Old, old, Master Shallow.

Shallow: Nay, she must be old; she cannot choose but be old; certain she's old; and had Robin Nightwork by old Nightwork before I came to Clement's Inn.

Silence: That's fifty-five year ago.

Shallow: Ha, cousin Silence, that thou hadst seen that that this knight and I have seen! Ha, Sir John, said I well?

Falstaff: We have heard the chimes at midnight, Master Shallow.

Shallow: That we have, that we have, that we have; in faith,
Sir John, we have: our watch-word was 'Hem boys!'
Come, let's to dinner; come, let's to dinner:
Jesus, the days that we have seen! Come, come.

Exeunt Falstaff and Justices

Bullcalf: Good Master Corporate Bardolph, stand my friend; and here's four Harry ten shillings in French crowns for you. In very truth, sir, I had as lief be hanged, sir, as go: and yet, for mine own part, sir, I do not care; but rather, because I am unwilling, and, for mine own part, have a desire to stay with my friends; else, sir, I did not care, for mine own part, so much.

Bardolph: Go to; stand aside.

Mouldy: And, good master corporal captain, for my old dame's sake, stand my friend: she has nobody to do any thing about her when I am gone; and she is old, and cannot help herself: You shall have forty, sir.

Bardolph: Go to; stand aside.

Feeble: By my troth, I care not; a man can die but once: we owe God a death: I'll ne'er bear a base mind: an't be my destiny, so; an't be not, so: no man is too good to serve's prince; and let it go which way it will, he that dies this year is quit for the next.

Bardolph: Well said; thou'rt a good fellow.

Feeble: Faith, I'll bear no base mind.

Re-enter Falstaff and the Justices

Falstaff: Come, sir, which men shall I have?

Shallow: Four of which you please.

Bardolph: Sir, a word with you: I have three pound to free Mouldy and Bullcalf.

Falstaff: Go to; well.

Shallow: Come, Sir John, which four will you have?

Falstaff: Do you choose for me.

Shallow: Marry, then, Mouldy, Bullcalf, Feeble and Shadow.

Falstaff: Mouldy and Bullcalf: for you, Mouldy, stay at home till you are past service: and for your part, Bullcalf, grow till you come unto it: I will none of you.

Shallow: Sir John, Sir John, do not yourself wrong: they are your likeliest men, and I would have you served with the best.

Falstaff: Will you tell me, Master Shallow, how to choose a man? Care I for the limb, the thewes, the stature, bulk, and big assemblance of a man! Give me the spirit, Master Shallow. Here's Wart; you see what a ragged appearance it is; a' shall charge you and discharge you with the motion of a pewterer's hammer, come off and on swifter than he that gibbets on the brewer's bucket. And this same half-faced fellow, Shadow; give me this man: he presents no mark to the enemy; the foeman may with as great aim level at the edge of a penknife. And for a retreat; how swiftly will this Feeble the woman's tailor run off! O, give me the spare men, and spare me the great ones. Put me a caliver into Wart's hand, Bardolph.

Bardolph: Hold, Wart, Traverse; thus, thus, thus.

Falstaff: Come, manage me your caliver. So: very well: go to: very good, exceeding good. O, give me always a little, lean, old, chapt, bald shot. Well said, i' faith, Wart; thou'rt a good scab: hold, there's a tester for thee.

Shallow: He is not his craft's master; he doth not do it right. I remember at Mile-end Green, when I lay at Clement's Inn- I was then Sir Dagonet in Arthur's show,- there was a little quiver fellow, and a' would manage you his piece thus; and a' would about and about, and come you in and come you in: 'rah, tah, tah,' would a' say; 'bounce' would a' say; and away again would a' go, and again would a' come: I shall ne'er see such a fellow.

Falstaff: These fellows will do well, Master Shallow. God keep you, Master Silence: I will not use many words with you. Fare you well, gentlemen both: I thank you: I must a dozen mile to-night. Bardolph, give the soldiers coats.

Shallow: Sir John, the Lord bless you! God prosper your affairs! God send us peace! At your return visit our house; let our old acquaintance be renewed; peradventure I will with ye to the court.

Falstaff: 'Fore God, I would you would, Master Shallow.

Shallow: Go to; I have spoke at a word. God keep you.

Falstaff: Fare you well, gentle gentlemen.

Exeunt Justices

On, Bardolph; lead the men away.

Exeunt Bardolph, Recruits, & c

As I return, I will fetch off these justices: I do see the bottom of Justice Shallow. Lord, Lord, how subject we old men are to this vice of lying! This same starved justice hath done nothing but prate to me of the wildness of his youth, and the feats he hath done about Turnbull Street: and every third word a lie, duer paid to the hearer than the Turk's tribute. I do remember him at Clement's Inn like a man made after supper of a cheese-paring: when a' was naked, he was, for all the world, like a forked radish, with a head fantastically carved upon it with a knife: a' was so forlorn, that his dimensions to any thick sight were invincible: a' was the very genius of famine; yet lecherous as a monkey, and the whores called him mandrake: a' came ever in the rearward of the fashion, and sung those tunes to the overscutched huswives that he heard the carmen whistle, and swear they were his fancies or his good-nights. And now is this Vice's dagger become a squire, and talks as familiarly of John a Gaunt as if he had been sworn brother to him; and I'll be sworn a' ne'er saw him but once in the Tilt-yard; and then he burst his head for crowding among the marshal's men. I saw it, and told John a Gaunt he beat his own name; for you might have thrust him and all his apparel into an eel-skin; the case of a treble hautboy was a mansion for him, a court: and now has he land and beefs. Well, I'll be acquainted with him, if I return; and it shall go hard but I will make him a philosopher's two stones to me: if the young dace be a bait for the old pike, I see no reason in the law of nature but I may snap at him. Let time shape, and there an end.

Exit

ACT IV

SCENE I

Yorkshire. Gaultree Forest

Enter the Archbishop of York, Mowbray, Lord Hastings, and others

Archbishop of York: What is this forest call'd?

Hastings: 'Tis Gaultree Forest, an't shall please your grace.

Archbishop of York: Here stand, my Lords; and send discoverers forth
To know the numbers of our enemies.

Hastings: We have sent forth already.

Archbishop of York: 'Tis well done.
My friends and brethren in these great affairs,
I must acquaint you that I have received
New-dated letters from Northumberland;
Their cold intent, tenor and substance, thus:
Here doth he wish his person, with such powers
As might hold sortance with his quality,
The which he could not levy; whereupon
He is retired, to ripe his growing fortunes,
To Scotland: and concludes in hearty prayers
That your attempts may overlive the hazard
And fearful melting of their opposite.

Mowbray: Thus do the hopes we have in him touch ground
And dash themselves to pieces.

Enter a Messenger

Hastings: Now, what news?

Messenger: West of this forest, scarcely off a mile,
In goodly form comes on the enemy;
And, by the ground they hide, I judge their number

Upon or near the rate of thirty thousand.
Mowbray: The just proportion that we gave them out
Let us sway on and face them in the field.
Archbishop of York: What well-appointed leader fronts us here?

Enter Westmoreland

Mowbray: I think it is my Lord of Westmoreland.
Westmoreland: Health and fair greeting from our general,
The prince, Lord John and Duke of Lancaster.
Archbishop of York: Say on, my Lord of Westmoreland, in peace:
What doth concern your coming?
Westmoreland: Then, my lord,
Unto your grace do I in chief address
The substance of my speech. If that rebellion
Came like itself, in base and abject routs,
Led on by bloody youth, guarded with rags,
And countenanced by boys and beggary,
I say, if damn'd commotion so appear'd,
In his true, native and most proper shape,
You, reverend father, and these noble lords
Had not been here, to dress the ugly form
Of base and bloody insurrection
With your fair honours. You, lord archbishop,
Whose see is by a civil peace maintained,
Whose beard the silver hand of peace hath touch'd,
Whose learning and good letters peace hath tutor'd,
Whose white investments figure innocence,
The dove and very blessed spirit of peace,
Wherefore do you so ill translate ourself
Out of the speech of peace that bears such grace,

Into the harsh and boisterous tongue of war;
Turning your books to graves, your ink to blood,
Your pens to lances and your tongue divine
To a trumpet and a point of war?
Archbishop of York: Wherefore do I this? so the question stands.
Briefly to this end: we are all diseased,
And with our surfeiting and wanton hours
Have brought ourselves into a burning fever,
And we must bleed for it; of which disease
Our late king, Richard, being infected, died.
But, my most noble Lord of Westmoreland,
I take not on me here as a physician,
Nor do I as an enemy to peace
Troop in the throngs of military men;
But rather show awhile like fearful war,
To diet rank minds sick of happiness
And purge the obstructions which begin to stop
Our very veins of life. Hear me more plainly.
I have in equal balance justly weigh'd
What wrongs our arms may do, what wrongs we suffer,
And find our griefs heavier than our offences.
We see which way the stream of time doth run,
And are enforced from our most quiet there
By the rough torrent of occasion;
And have the summary of all our griefs,
When time shall serve, to show in articles;
Which long ere this we offer'd to the king,
And might by no suit gain our audience:
When we are wrong'd and would unfold our griefs,

We are denied access unto his person
Even by those men that most have done us wrong.
The dangers of the days but newly gone,
Whose memory is written on the earth
With yet appearing blood, and the examples
Of every minute's instance, present now,
Hath put us in these ill-beseeming arms,
Not to break peace or any branch of it,
But to establish here a peace indeed,
Concurring both in name and quality.

Westmoreland: When ever yet was your appeal denied?
Wherein have you been galled by the king?
What peer hath been suborn'd to grate on you,
That you should seal this lawless bloody book
Of forged rebellion with a seal divine
And consecrate commotion's bitter edge?

Archbishop of York: My brother general, the commonwealth,
To brother born an household cruelty,
I make my quarrel in particular.

Westmoreland: There is no need of any such redress;
Or if there were, it not belongs to you.

Mowbray: Why not to him in part, and to us all
That feel the bruises of the days before,
And suffer the condition of these times
To lay a heavy and unequal hand
Upon our honours?

Westmoreland: O, my good Lord Mowbray,
Construe the times to their necessities,
And you shall say indeed, it is the time,
And not the king, that doth you injuries.

Yet for your part, it not appears to me
Either from the king or in the present time
That you should have an inch of any ground
To build a grief on: were you not restored
To all the Duke of Norfolk's signories,
Your noble and right well remember'd father's?

Mowbray: What thing, in honour, had my father lost,
That need to be revived and breathed in me?
The king that loved him, as the state stood then,
Was force perforce compell'd to banish him:
And then that Harry Bolingbroke and he,
Being mounted and both roused in their seats,
Their neighing coursers daring of the spur,
Their armed staves in charge, their beavers down,
Their eyes of fire sparking through sights of steel
And the loud trumpet blowing them together,
Then, then, when there was nothing could have stay'd
My father from the breast of Bolingbroke,
O when the king did throw his warder down,
His own life hung upon the staff he threw;
Then threw he down himself and all their lives
That by indictment and by dint of sword
Have since miscarried under Bolingbroke.

Westmoreland: You speak, Lord Mowbray, now you know not what.
The Earl of Hereford was reputed then
In England the most valiant gentlemen:
Who knows on whom fortune would then have smiled?
But if your father had been victor there,
He ne'er had borne it out of Coventry:

For all the country in a general voice
Cried hate upon him; and all their prayers and love
Were set on Hereford, whom they doted on
And bless'd and graced indeed, more than the king.
But this is mere digression from my purpose.
Here come I from our princely general
To know your griefs; to tell you from his grace
That he will give you audience; and wherein
It shall appear that your demands are just,
You shall enjoy them, every thing set off
That might so much as think you enemies.

Mowbray: But he hath forced us to compel this offer;
And it proceeds from policy, not love.

Westmoreland: Mowbray, you overween to take it so;
This offer comes from mercy, not from fear:
For, lo! within a ken our army lies,
Upon mine honour, all too confident
To give admittance to a thought of fear.
Our battle is more full of names than yours,
Our men more perfect in the use of arms,
Our armour all as strong, our cause the best;
Then reason will our heart should be as good
Say you not then our offer is compell'd.

Mowbray: Well, by my will we shall admit no parley.

Westmoreland: That argues but the shame of your offence:
A rotten case abides no handling.

Hastings: Hath the Prince John a full commission,
In very ample virtue of his father,
To hear and absolutely to determine
Of what conditions we shall stand upon?

Westmoreland: That is intended in the general's name:
I muse you make so slight a question.

Archbishop of York: Then take, my Lord of Westmoreland, this schedule,
For this contains our general grievances:
Each several article herein redress'd,
All members of our cause, both here and hence,
That are insinew'd to this action,
Acquitted by a true substantial form
And present execution of our wills
To us and to our purposes confined,
We come within our awful banks again
And knit our powers to the arm of peace.

Westmoreland: This will I show the general. Please you, Lords,
In sight of both our battles we may meet;
And either end in peace, which God so frame!
Or to the place of difference call the swords
Which must decide it.

Archbishop of York: My lord, we will do so.

Exit Westmoreland

Mowbray: There is a thing within my bosom tells me
That no conditions of our peace can stand.

Hastings: Fear you not that: if we can make our peace
Upon such large terms and so absolute
As our conditions shall consist upon,
Our peace shall stand as firm as rocky mountains.

Mowbray: Yea, but our valuation shall be such
That every slight and false-derived cause,
Yea, every idle, nice and wanton reason

Shall to the king taste of this action;
That, were our royal faiths martyrs in love,
We shall be winnow'd with so rough a wind
That even our corn shall seem as light as chaff
And good from bad find no partition.

Archbishop of York: No, no, my lord. Note this; the king is weary
Of dainty and such picking grievances:
For he hath found to end one doubt by death
Revives two greater in the heirs of life,
And therefore will he wipe his tables clean
And keep no tell-tale to his memory
That may repeat and history his loss
To new remembrance; for full well he knows
He cannot so precisely weed this land
As his misdoubts present occasion:
His foes are so enrooted with his friends
That, plucking to unfix an enemy,
He doth unfasten so and shake a friend:
So that this land, like an offensive wife
That hath enraged him on to offer strokes,
As he is striking, holds his infant up
And hangs resolved correction in the arm
That was uprear'd to execution.

Hastings: Besides, the king hath wasted all his rods
On late offenders, that he now doth lack
The very instruments of chastisement:
So that his power, like to a Fangless lion,
May offer, but not hold.

Archbishop of York: 'Tis very true:
And therefore be assured, my good lord marshal,

If we do now make our atonement well,
Our peace will, like a broken limb united,
Grow stronger for the breaking.

Mowbray: Be it so.
Here is return'd my Lord of Westmoreland.

Re-enter Westmoreland

Westmoreland: The prince is here at hand: pleaseth your lordship
To meet his grace just distance 'tween our armies.

Mowbray: Your grace of York, in God's name then, set forward.

Archbishop of York: Before, and greet his grace: my lord, we come.

Exeunt

SCENE II

Another part of the forest

Enter, from one side, Mowbray, attended; afterwards the Archbishop of York, Hastings, and others: from the other side, Prince John of Lancaster, and Westmoreland; Officers, and others with them

Lancaster: You are well encounter'd here, my cousin Mowbray:
Good day to you, gentle Lord Archbishop;
And so to you, Lord Hastings, and to all.
My Lord of York, it better show'd with you
When that your flock, assembled by the bell,
Encircled you to hear with reverence
Your exposition on the holy text
Than now to see you here an iron man,
Cheering a rout of rebels with your drum,
Turning the word to sword and life to death.
That man that sits within a monarch's heart,
And ripens in the sunshine of his favour,
Would he abuse the countenance of the king,
Alack, what mischiefs might he set abrooch
In shadow of such greatness! With you, lord bishop,
It is even so. Who hath not heard it spoken
How deep you were within the books of God?
To us the speaker in his parliament;
To us the imagined voice of God himself;
The very opener and intelligencer
Between the grace, the sanctities of heaven
And our dull workings. O, who shall believe

But you misuse the reverence of your place,
Employ the countenance and grace of heaven,
As a false favourite doth his prince's name,
In deeds dishonourable? You have ta'en up,
Under the counterfeited zeal of God,
The subjects of his substitute, my father,
And both against the peace of heaven and him
Have here up-swarm'd them.

Archbishop of York: Good my Lord of Lancaster,
I am not here against your father's peace;
But, as I told my Lord of Westmoreland,
The time misorder'd doth, in common sense,
Crowd us and crush us to this monstrous form,
To hold our safety up. I sent your grace
The parcels and particulars of our grief,
The which hath been with scorn shoved from the court,
Whereon this Hydra son of war is born;
Whose dangerous eyes may well be charm'd asleep
With grant of our most just and right desires,
And true obedience, of this madness cured,
Stoop tamely to the foot of majesty.

Mowbray: If not, we ready are to try our fortunes
To the last man.

Hastings: And though we here fall down,
We have supplies to second our attempt:
If they miscarry, theirs shall second them;
And so success of mischief shall be born
And heir from heir shall hold this quarrel up
Whiles England shall have generation.

Lancaster: You are too Shallow, Hastings, much too Shallow,
To sound the bottom of the after-times.

Westmoreland: Pleaseth your grace to answer them directly
How far forth you do like their articles.

Lancaster: I like them all, and do allow them well,
And swear here, by the honour of my blood,
My father's purposes have been mistook,
And some about him have too lavishly
Wrested his meaning and authority.
My lord, these griefs shall be with speed redress'd;
Upon my soul, they shall. If this may please you,
Discharge your powers unto their several counties,
As we will ours: and here between the armies
Let's drink together friendly and embrace,
That all their eyes may bear those tokens home
Of our restored love and amity.

Archbishop of York: I take your princely word for these redresses.

Lancaster: I give it you, and will maintain my word:
And thereupon I drink unto your grace.

Hastings: Go, captain, and deliver to the army
This news of peace: let them have pay, and part:
I know it will well please them. Hie thee, captain.

Exit Officer

Archbishop of York: To you, my noble Lord of Westmoreland.

Westmoreland: I pledge your grace; and, if you knew what pains
I have bestow'd to breed this present peace,
You would drink freely: but my love to ye
Shall show itself more openly hereafter.

Archbishop of York: I do not doubt you.

Westmoreland: I am glad of it.
Health to my Lord and gentle cousin, Mowbray.
Mowbray: You wish me health in very happy season;
For I am, on the sudden, something ill.
Archbishop of York: Against ill chances men are ever merry;
But heaviness foreruns the good event.
Westmoreland: Therefore be merry, coz; since sudden sorrow
Serves to say thus, 'some good thing comes to-morrow.'
Archbishop of York: Believe me, I am passing light in spirit.
Mowbray: So much the worse, if your own rule be true.

Shouts within

Lancaster: The word of peace is render'd: hark, how they shout!
Mowbray: This had been cheerful after victory.
Archbishop of York: A peace is of the nature of a conquest;
For then both parties nobly are subdued,
And neither party loser.
Lancaster: Go, my lord,
And let our army be discharged too.

Exit Westmoreland

And, good my lord, so please you, let our trains
March, by us, that we may peruse the men
We should have coped withal.
Archbishop of York: Go, good Lord Hastings,
And, ere they be dismissed, let them march by.

Exit Hastings

Lancaster: I trust, lords, we shall lie to-night together.

Re-enter Westmoreland

Now, cousin, wherefore stands our army still?

Westmoreland: The leaders, having charge from you to stand,
Will not go off until they hear you speak.

Lancaster: They know their duties.

Re-enter Hastings

Hastings: My lord, our army is dispersed already;
Like youthful steers unyoked, they take their courses
East, west, north, south; or, like a school broke up,
Each hurries toward his home and sporting-place.

Westmoreland: Good tidings, my Lord Hastings; for the which
I do arrest thee, traitor, of high treason:
And you, lord archbishop, and you, Lord Mowbray,
Of capitol treason I attach you both.

Mowbray: Is this proceeding just and honourable?

Westmoreland: Is your assembly so?

Archbishop of York: Will you thus break your faith?

Lancaster: I pawn'd thee none:
I promised you redress of these same grievances
Whereof you did complain; which, by mine honour,
I will perform with a most Christian care.
But for you, rebels, look to taste the due
Meet for rebellion and such acts as yours.
Most shallowly did you these arms commence,
Fondly brought here and foolishly sent hence.
Strike up our drums, pursue the scatter'd stray:
God, and not we, hath safely fought to-day.
Some guard these traitors to the block of death,
Treason's true bed and yielder up of breath.

Exeunt

SCENE III

Another part of the forest

Alarum. Excursions. Enter Falstaff and Colevile, meeting

Falstaff: What's your name, sir? of what condition are you, and of what place, I pray?

Colevile: I am a knight, sir, and my name is Colevile of the Dale.

Falstaff: Well, then, Colevile is your name, a knight is your degree, and your place the dale: Colevile shall be still your name, a traitor your degree, and the dungeon your place, a place deep enough; so shall you be still Colevile of the dale.

Colevile: Are not you Sir John Falstaff?

Falstaff: As good a man as he, sir, whoe'er I am. Do ye yield, sir? or shall I sweat for you? if I do sweat, they are the drops of thy lovers, and they weep for thy death: therefore rouse up fear and trembling, and do observance to my mercy.

Colevile: I think you are Sir John Falstaff, and in that thought yield me.

Falstaff: I have a whole school of tongues in this belly of mine, and not a tongue of them all speaks any other word but my name. An I had but a belly of any indifference, I were simply the most active fellow in Europe: my womb, my womb, my womb, undoes me.

Here comes our general.

Enter Prince John of Lancaster, Westmoreland, Blunt, and others

Lancaster: The heat is past; follow no further now:
Call in the powers, good cousin Westmoreland.

Exit Westmoreland

Now, Falstaff, where have you been all this while?
When every thing is ended, then you come:
These tardy tricks of yours will, on my life,
One time or other break some gallows' back.

Falstaff: I would be sorry, my Lord, but it should be thus: I never knew yet but rebuke and cheque was the reward of valour. Do you think me a swallow, an arrow, or a bullet? have I, in my poor and old motion, the expedition of thought? I have speeded hither with the very extremest inch of possibility; I have foundered nine score and odd posts: and here, travel-tainted as I am, have in my pure and immaculate valour, taken Sir John Colevile of the dale, a most furious knight and valorous enemy. But what of that? he saw me, and yielded; that I may justly say, with the hook-nosed fellow of Rome, 'I came, saw, and overcame.'

Lancaster: It was more of his courtesy than your deserving.

Falstaff: I know not: here he is, and here I yield him: and I beseech your grace, let it be booked with the rest of this day's deeds; or, by the Lord, I will have it in a particular ballad else, with mine own picture on the top on't, Colevile kissing my foot: to the which course if I be enforced, if you do not all show like gilt twopences to me, and I in the clear sky of fame o'ershine you as much as the full moon doth the cinders of the element, which show like pins' heads to her, believe not the word of the noble: therefore let me have right, and let desert mount.

Lancaster: Thine's too heavy to mount.

Falstaff: Let it shine, then.

Lancaster: Thine's too thick to shine.

Falstaff: Let it do something, my good Lord, that may do me good, and call it what you will.

Lancaster: Is thy name Colevile?

Colevile: It is, my Lord.

Lancaster: A famous rebel art thou, Colevile.

Falstaff: And a famous true subject took him.

Colevile: I am, my lord, but as my betters are
That led me hither: had they been ruled by me,
You should have won them dearer than you have.

Falstaff: I know not how they sold themselves: but thou, like a kind fellow, gavest thyself away gratis; and I thank thee for thee.

Re-enter Westmoreland

Lancaster: Now, have you left pursuit?

Westmoreland: Retreat is made and execution stay'd.

Lancaster: Send Colevile with his confederates
To York, to present execution:
Blunt, lead him hence; and see you guard him sure.

Exeunt Blunt and others with Colevile

And now dispatch we toward the court, my lords:
I hear the king my father is sore sick:
Our news shall go before us to his majesty,
Which, cousin, you shall bear to comfort him,

And we with sober speed will follow you.

Falstaff: My Lord, I beseech you, give me leave to go
Through Gloucestershire: and, when you come to court,
Stand my good Lord, pray, in your good report.

Lancaster: Fare you well, Falstaff: I, in my condition,
Shall better speak of you than you deserve.

Exeunt all but Falstaff

Falstaff: I would you had but the wit: 'twere better than your dukedom. Good faith, this same young sober-blooded boy doth not love me; nor a man cannot make him laugh; but that's no marvel, he drinks no wine. There's never none of these demure boys come to any proof; for thin drink doth so over-cool their blood, and making many fish-meals, that they fall into a kind of male green-sickness; and then when they marry, they get wenches: they are generally fools and cowards; which some of us should be too, but for inflammation. A good sherris sack hath a two-fold operation in it. It ascends me into the brain; dries me there all the foolish and dull and curdy vapours which environ it; makes it apprehensive, quick, forgetive, full of nimble fiery and delectable shapes, which, delivered o'er to the voice, the tongue, which is the birth, becomes excellent wit. The second property of your excellent sherris is, the warming of the blood; which, before cold and settled, left the liver white and pale, which is the badge of pusillanimity and cowardice; but the sherris warms it and makes it course from the inwards to the parts extreme: it illumineth the face, which as a beacon gives warning to all the rest of this little kingdom, man, to arm; and then the vital commoners and inland petty spirits muster me all to their captain, the heart, who, great and puffed up with this retinue, doth any deed of courage; and this valour comes of sherris. So that skill in the weapon is nothing without sack, for that sets it a-work; and learning a mere hoard of gold kept by a devil, till sack commences it and sets it in act and use. Hereof comes it that Prince Harry is valiant; for the cold blood he did naturally inherit of his father, he hath, like lean, sterile and bare land, manured, husbanded and tilled with excellent endeavour of drinking good and good store of fertile sherris, that he is become very hot and valiant. If I had a thousand sons, the first humane principle I would teach them should be, to forswear thin potations and to addict themselves to sack.

Enter Bardolph

How now Bardolph?

Bardolph: The army is discharged all and gone.

Falstaff: Let them go. I'll through Gloucestershire; and there will I visit Master Robert Shallow, esquire: I have him already tempering between my finger and my thumb, and shortly will I seal with him. Come away.

Exeunt

SCENE IV

Westminster. The Jerusalem Chamber

Enter King Henry IV, the Princes Thomas of Clarence and Humphrey of Gloucester, Warwick, and others

King Henry IV: Now, Lords, if God doth give successful end
To this debate that bleedeth at our doors,
We will our youth lead on to higher fields
And draw no swords but what are sanctified.
Our navy is address'd, our power collected,
Our substitutes in absence well invested,
And every thing lies level to our wish:
Only, we want a little personal strength;
And pause us, till these rebels, now afoot,
Come underneath the yoke of government.

Warwick: Both which we doubt not but your majesty
Shall soon enjoy.

King Henry IV: Humphrey, my son of Gloucester,
Where is the prince your brother?

Gloucester: I think he's gone to hunt, my Lord, at Windsor.

King Henry IV: And how accompanied?

Gloucester: I do not know, my Lord.

King Henry IV: Is not his brother, Thomas of Clarence, with him?

Gloucester: No, my good lord; he is in presence here.

Clarence: What would my lord and father?

King Henry IV: Nothing but well to thee, Thomas of Clarence.
How chance thou art not with the prince thy brother?
He loves thee, and thou dost neglect him, Thomas;
Thou hast a better place in his affection

Than all thy brothers: cherish it, my boy,
And noble offices thou mayst effect
Of mediation, after I am dead,
Between his greatness and thy other brethren:
Therefore omit him not; Blunt not his love,
Nor lose the good advantage of his grace
By seeming cold or careless of his will;
For he is gracious, if he be observed:
He hath a tear for pity and a hand
Open as day for melting charity:
Yet notwithstanding, being incensed, he's flint,
As humorous as winter and as sudden
As flaws congealed in the spring of day.
His temper, therefore, must be well observed:
Chide him for faults, and do it reverently,
When thou perceive his blood inclined to mirth;
But, being moody, give him line and scope,
Till that his passions, like a whale on ground,
Confound themselves with working. Learn this, Thomas,
And thou shalt prove a shelter to thy friends,
A hoop of gold to bind thy brothers in,
That the united vessel of their blood,
Mingled with venom of suggestion-
As, force perforce, the age will pour it in-
Shall never leak, though it do work as strong
As aconitum or rash gunpowder.

Clarence: I shall observe him with all care and love.

King Henry IV: Why art thou not at Windsor with him, Thomas?

Clarence: He is not there to-day; he dines in London.

King Henry IV: And how accompanied? canst thou tell that?
Clarence: With Poins, and other his continual followers.
King Henry IV: Most subject is the fattest soil to weeds;
And he, the noble image of my youth,
Is overspread with them: therefore my grief
Stretches itself beyond the hour of death:
The blood weeps from my heart when I do shape
In forms imaginary the unguided days
And rotten times that you shall look upon
When I am sleeping with my ancestors.
For when his headstrong riot hath no curb,
When rage and hot blood are his counsellors,
When means and lavish manners meet together,
O, with what wings shall his affections fly
Towards fronting peril and opposed decay!
Warwick: My gracious Lord, you look beyond him quite:
The prince but studies his companions
Like a strange tongue, wherein, to gain the language,
'Tis needful that the most immodest word
Be look'd upon and learn'd; which once attain'd,
Your highness knows, comes to no further use
But to be known and hated. So, like gross terms,
The prince will in the perfectness of time
Cast off his followers; and their memory
Shall as a pattern or a measure live,
By which his grace must mete the lives of others,
Turning past evils to advantages.
King Henry IV: 'Tis seldom when the bee doth leave her comb
In the dead carrion.

Enter Westmoreland

Who's here? Westmoreland?
Westmoreland: Health to my sovereign, and new happiness
Added to that that I am to deliver!
Prince John your son doth kiss your grace's hand:
Mowbray, the Bishop Scroop, Hastings and all
Are brought to the correction of your law;
There is not now a rebel's sword unsheath'd
But peace puts forth her olive every where.
The manner how this action hath been borne
Here at more leisure may your highness read,
With every course in his particular.
King Henry IV: O Westmoreland, thou art a summer bird,
Which ever in the haunch of winter sings
The lifting up of day.

Enter Harcourt

Look, here's more news.
Harcourt: From enemies heaven keep your majesty;
And, when they stand against you, may they fall
As those that I am come to tell you of!
The Earl Northumberland and the Lord Bardolph,
With a great power of English and of Scots
Are by the sheriff of Yorkshire overthrown:
The manner and true order of the fight
This packet, please it you, contains at large.
King Henry IV: And wherefore should these good news make me sick?
Will fortune never come with both hands full,
But write her fair words still in foulest letters?

She either gives a stomach and no food;
Such are the poor, in health; or else a feast
And takes away the stomach; such are the rich,
That have abundance and enjoy it not.
I should rejoice now at this happy news;
And now my sight fails, and my brain is giddy:
O me! come near me; now I am much ill.

Gloucester: Comfort, your majesty!

Clarence: O my royal father!

Westmoreland: My sovereign lord, cheer up yourself, look up.

Warwick: Be patient, princes; you do know, these fits
Are with his highness very ordinary.
Stand from him. Give him air; he'll straight be well.

Clarence: No, no, he cannot long hold out these pangs:
The incessant care and labour of his mind
Hath wrought the mure that should confine it in
So thin that life looks through and will break out.

Gloucester: The people fear me; for they do observe
Unfather'd heirs and loathly births of nature:
The seasons change their manners, as the year
Had found some months asleep and leap'd them over.

Clarence: The river hath thrice flow'd, no ebb between;
And the old folk, time's doting chronicles,
Say it did so a little time before
That our great-grandsire, Edward, sick'd and died.

Warwick: Speak lower, princes, for the king recovers.

Gloucester: This apoplexy will certain be his end.

King Henry IV: I pray you, take me up, and bear me hence
Into some other chamber: softly, pray.

SCENE V

Another chamber

King Henry IV lying on a bed: Clarence, Gloucester, Warwick, and others in attendance

King Henry IV: Let there be no noise made, my gentle friends;
Unless some dull and favourable hand
Will whisper music to my weary spirit.

Warwick: Call for the music in the other room.

King Henry IV: Set me the crown upon my pillow here.

Clarence: His eye is hollow, and he changes much.

Warwick: Less noise, less noise!

Enter Prince Henry

Prince Henry: Who saw the Duke of Clarence?

Clarence: I am here, brother, full of heaviness.

Prince Henry: How now! rain within doors, and none abroad!
How doth the king?

Gloucester: Exceeding ill.

Prince Henry: Heard he the good news yet?
Tell it him.

Gloucester: He alter'd much upon the hearing it.

Prince Henry: If he be sick with joy, he'll recover without physic.

Warwick: Not so much noise, my lords: sweet prince, speak low;
The king your father is disposed to sleep.

Clarence: Let us withdraw into the other room.

Warwick: Will't please your grace to go along with us?

Prince Henry: No; I will sit and watch here by the king.

Exeunt all but Prince Henry

Why doth the crown lie there upon his pillow,
Being so troublesome a bedfellow?
O polish'd perturbation! golden care!
That keep'st the ports of slumber open wide
To many a watchful night! sleep with it now!
Yet not so sound and half so deeply sweet
As he whose brow with homely biggen bound
Snores out the watch of night. O majesty!
When thou dost pinch thy bearer, thou dost sit
Like a rich armour worn in heat of day,
That scalds with safety. By his gates of breath
There lies a downy feather which stirs not:
Did he suspire, that light and weightless down
Perforce must move. My gracious lord! my father!
This sleep is sound indeed, this is a sleep
That from this golden rigol hath divorced
So many English kings. Thy due from me
Is tears and heavy sorrows of the blood,
Which nature, love, and filial tenderness,
Shall, O dear father, pay thee plenteously:
My due from thee is this imperial crown,
Which, as immediate as thy place and blood,
Derives itself to me. Lo, here it sits,
Which God shall guard: and put the world's whole strength
Into one giant arm, it shall not force
This lineal honour from me: this from thee
Will I to mine leave, as 'tis left to me.

Exit

King Henry IV: Warwick! Gloucester! Clarence!

Re-enter Warwick, Gloucester, Clarence, and the rest

Clarence: Doth the king call?

Warwick: What would your majesty? How fares your grace?

King Henry IV: Why did you leave me here alone, my Lords?

Clarence: We left the prince my brother here, my liege,
Who undertook to sit and watch by you.

King Henry IV: The Prince of Wales! Where is he? let me see him:
He is not here.

Warwick: This door is open; he is gone this way.

Gloucester: He came not through the chamber where we stay'd.

King Henry IV: Where is the crown? who took it from my pillow?

Warwick: When we withdrew, my liege, we left it here.

King Henry IV: The prince hath ta'en it hence: go, seek him out.
Is he so hasty that he doth suppose
My sleep my death?
Find him, my Lord of Warwick; chide him hither.

Exit Warwick

This part of his conjoins with my disease,
And helps to end me. See, sons, what things you are!
How quickly nature falls into revolt
When gold becomes her object!
For this the foolish over-careful fathers
Have broke their sleep with thoughts, their brains with care,
Their bones with industry;
For this they have engrossed and piled up
The canker'd heaps of strange-achieved gold;
For this they have been thoughtful to invest

Their sons with arts and martial exercises:
When, like the bee, culling from every flower
The virtuous sweets,
Our thighs pack'd with wax, our mouths with honey,
We bring it to the hive, and, like the bees,
Are murdered for our pains. This bitter taste
Yield his engrossments to the ending father.

Re-enter Warwick

Now, where is he that will not stay so long
Till his friend sickness hath determined me?

Warwick: My Lord, I found the prince in the next room,
Washing with kindly tears his gentle cheeks,
With such a deep demeanor in great sorrow
That tyranny, which never quaff'd but blood,
Would, by beholding him, have wash'd his knife
With gentle eye-drops. He is coming hither.

King Henry IV: But wherefore did he take away the crown?

Re-enter Prince Henry

Lo, where he comes. Come hither to me, Harry.
Depart the chamber, leave us here alone.

Exeunt Warwick and the rest

Prince Henry: I never thought to hear you speak again.

King Henry IV: Thy wish was father, Harry, to that thought:
I stay too long by thee, I weary thee.
Dost thou so hunger for mine empty chair
That thou wilt needs invest thee with my honours
Before thy hour be ripe? O foolish youth!
Thou seek'st the greatness that will o'erwhelm thee.

Stay but a little; for my cloud of dignity
Is held from falling with so weak a wind
That it will quickly drop: my day is dim.
Thou hast stolen that which after some few hours
Were thine without offence; and at my death
Thou hast seal'd up my expectation:
Thy life did manifest thou lovedst me not,
And thou wilt have me die assured of it.
Thou hidest a thousand daggers in thy thoughts,
Which thou hast whetted on thy stony heart,
To stab at half an hour of my life.
What! canst thou not forbear me half an hour?
Then get thee gone and dig my grave thyself,
And bid the merry bells ring to thine ear
That thou art crowned, not that I am dead.
Let all the tears that should bedew my hearse
Be drops of balm to sanctify thy head:
Only compound me with forgotten dust
Give that which gave thee life unto the worms.
Pluck down my officers, break my decrees;
For now a time is come to mock at form:
Harry the Fifth is crown'd: up, vanity!
Down, royal state! all you sage counsellors, hence!
And to the English court assemble now,
From every region, apes of idleness!
Now, neighbour confines, purge you of your scum:
Have you a ruffian that will swear, drink, dance,
Revel the night, rob, murder, and commit
The oldest sins the newest kind of ways?
Be happy, he will trouble you no more;

England shall double gild his treble guilt,
England shall give him office, honour, might;
For the fifth Harry from curb'd licence plucks
The muzzle of restraint, and the wild dog
Shall flesh his tooth on every innocent.
O my poor kingdom, sick with civil blows!
When that my care could not withhold thy riots,
What wilt thou do when riot is thy care?
O, thou wilt be a wilderness again,
Peopled with wolves, thy old inhabitants!

Prince Henry: O, pardon me, my liege! but for my tears,
The moist impediments unto my speech,
I had forestall'd this dear and deep rebuke
Ere you with grief had spoke and I had heard
The course of it so far. There is your crown;
And He that wears the crown immortally
Long guard it yours! If I affect it more
Than as your honour and as your renown,
Let me no more from this obedience rise,
Which my most inward true and duteous spirit
Teacheth, this prostrate and exterior bending.
God witness with me, when I here came in,
And found no course of breath within your majesty,
How cold it struck my heart! If I do feign,
O, let me in my present wildness die
And never live to show the incredulous world
The noble change that I have purposed!
Coming to look on you, thinking you dead,
And dead almost, my liege, to think you were,
I spake unto this crown as having sense,

And thus upbraided it: 'The care on thee depending
Hath fed upon the body of my father;
Therefore, thou best of gold art worst of gold:
Other, less fine in carat, is more precious,
Preserving life in medicine potable;
But thou, most fine, most honour'd: most renown'd,
Hast eat thy bearer up.' Thus, my most royal liege,
Accusing it, I put it on my head,
To try with it, as with an enemy
That had before my face murder'd my father,
The quarrel of a true inheritor.
But if it did infect my blood with joy,
Or swell my thoughts to any strain of pride;
If any rebel or vain spirit of mine
Did with the least affection of a welcome
Give entertainment to the might of it,
Let God for ever keep it from my head
And make me as the poorest vassal is
That doth with awe and terror kneel to it!

King Henry IV: O my son,
God put it in thy mind to take it hence,
That thou mightst win the more thy father's love,
Pleading so wisely in excuse of it!
Come hither, Harry, sit thou by my bed;
And hear, I think, the very latest counsel
That ever I shall breathe. God knows, my son,
By what by-paths and indirect crook'd ways
I met this crown; and I myself know well
How troublesome it sat upon my head.
To thee it shall descend with bitter quiet,

Better opinion, better confirmation;
For all the soil of the achievement goes
With me into the earth. It seem'd in me
But as an honour snatch'd with boisterous hand,
And I had many living to upbraid
My gain of it by their assistances;
Which daily grew to quarrel and to bloodshed,
Wounding supposed peace: all these bold fears
Thou see'st with peril I have answered;
For all my reign hath been but as a scene
Acting that argument: and now my death
Changes the mode; for what in me was purchased,
Falls upon thee in a more fairer sort;
So thou the garland wear'st successively.
Yet, though thou stand'st more sure than I could do,
Thou art not firm enough, since griefs are green;
And all my friends, which thou must make thy friends,
Have but their stings and teeth newly ta'en out;
By whose fell working I was first advanced
And by whose power I well might lodge a fear
To be again displaced: which to avoid,
I cut them off; and had a purpose now
To lead out many to the Holy Land,
Lest rest and lying still might make them look
Too near unto my state. Therefore, my Harry,
Be it thy course to busy giddy minds
With foreign quarrels; that action, hence borne out,
May waste the memory of the former days.
More would I, but my lungs are wasted so

That strength of speech is utterly denied me.
How I came by the crown, O God forgive;
And grant it may with thee in true peace live!

Prince Henry: My gracious liege,
You won it, wore it, kept it, gave it me;
Then plain and right must my possession be:
Which I with more than with a common pain
'Gainst all the world will rightfully maintain.

Enter Lord John of Lancaster

King Henry IV: Look, look, here comes my John of Lancaster.

Lancaster: Health, peace, and happiness to my royal father!

King Henry IV: Thou bring'st me happiness and peace, son John;
But health, alack, with youthful wings is flown
From this bare wither'd trunk: upon thy sight
My worldly business makes a period.
Where is my Lord of Warwick?

Prince Henry: My Lord of Warwick!

Enter Warwick, and others

King Henry IV: Doth any name particular belong
Unto the lodging where I first did swoon?

Warwick: 'Tis call'd Jerusalem, my noble lord.

King Henry IV: Laud be to God! even there my life must end.
It hath been prophesied to me many years,
I should not die but in Jerusalem;
Which vainly I supposed the Holy Land:
But bear me to that chamber; there I'll lie;
In that Jerusalem shall Harry die.

Exeunt

ACT V

SCENE I

Gloucestershire. Shallow's house

Enter Shallow, Falstaff, Bardolph, and Page

Shallow: By cock and pie, sir, you shall not away to-night. What, Davy, I say!

Falstaff: You must excuse me, Master Robert Shallow.

Shallow: I will not excuse you; you shall not be excused; excuses shall not be admitted; there is no excuse shall serve; you shall not be excused. Why, Davy!

Enter Davy

Davy: Here, sir.

Shallow: Davy, Davy, Davy, Davy, let me see, Davy; let me see, Davy; let me see: yea, marry, William cook, bid him come hither. Sir John, you shall not be excused.

Davy: Marry, sir, thus; those precepts cannot be served: and, again, sir, shall we sow the headland with wheat?

Shallow: With red wheat, Davy. But for William cook: are there no young pigeons?

Davy: Yes, sir. Here is now the smith's note for shoeing and plough-irons.

Shallow: Let it be cast and paid. Sir John, you shall not be excused.

Davy: Now, sir, a new link to the bucket must need be had: and, sir, do you mean to stop any of William's wages, about the sack he lost the other day at Hinckley fair?

Shallow: A' shall answer it. Some pigeons, Davy, a couple of short-legged hens, a joint of mutton, and any pretty little tiny kickshaws, tell William cook.

Davy: Doth the man of war stay all night, sir?

Shallow: Yea, Davy. I will use him well: a friend i' the court is better than a penny in purse. Use his men well, Davy; for they are arrant knaves, and will backbite.

Davy: No worse than they are backbitten, sir; for they have marvellous foul linen.

Shallow: Well conceited, Davy: about thy business, Davy.

Davy: I beseech you, sir, to countenance William Visor of Woncot against Clement Perkes of the hill.

Shallow: There is many complaints, Davy, against that Visor: that Visor is an arrant knave, on my knowledge.

Davy: I grant your worship that he is a knave, sir; but yet, God forbid, sir, but a knave should have some countenance at his friend's request. An honest man, sir, is able to speak for himself, when a knave is not. I have served your worship truly, sir, this eight years; and if I cannot once or twice in a quarter bear out a knave against an honest man, I have but a very little credit with your worship. The knave is mine honest friend, sir; therefore, I beseech your worship, let him be countenanced.

Shallow: Go to; I say he shall have no wrong. Look about, Davy.

Exit Davy

Where are you, Sir John? Come, come, come, off

with your boots. Give me your hand, Master Bardolph.

Bardolph: I am glad to see your worship.

Shallow: I thank thee with all my heart, kind
Master Bardolph: and welcome, my tall fellow.

To the Page

Come, Sir John.

Falstaff: I'll follow you, good Master Robert Shallow.

Exit Shallow

Bardolph, look to our horses.

Exeunt Bardolph and Page

If I were sawed into quantities, I should make four dozen of such bearded hermits' staves as Master Shallow. It is a wonderful thing to see the semblable coherence of his men's spirits and his: they, by observing of him, do bear themselves like foolish justices; he, by conversing with them, is turned into a justice-like serving-man: their spirits are so married in conjunction with the participation of society that they flock together in consent, like so many wild-geese. If I had a suit to Master Shallow, I would humour his men with the imputation of being near their master: if to his men, I would curry with Master Shallow that no man could better command his servants. It is certain that either wise bearing or ignorant carriage is caught, as men take diseases, one of another: therefore let men take heed of their company. I will devise matter enough out of this Shallow to keep Prince Harry in continual laughter the wearing out of six fashions, which is four terms, or two actions, and a' shall laugh without intervallums. O, it is much that a lie with a slight oath and a jest with a sad brow will do with a fellow that never had the ache in his shoulders! O, you shall see him laugh till his face be like a wet cloak ill laid up!

Shallow*[Within]*: Sir John!

Falstaff: I come, Master Shallow; I come, Master Shallow.

Exit

SCENE II

Westminster. The palace

Enter Warwick and the Lord Chief-Justice, meeting

Warwick: How now, my Lord Chief-Justice! whither away?

Lord Chief-Justice: How doth the king?

Warwick: Exceeding well; his cares are now all ended.

Lord Chief-Justice: I hope, not dead.

Warwick: He's walk'd the way of nature;
And to our purposes he lives no more.

Lord Chief-Justice: I would his majesty had call'd me with him:
The service that I truly did his life
Hath left me open to all injuries.

Warwick: Indeed I think the young king loves you not.

Lord Chief-Justice: I know he doth not, and do arm myself
To welcome the condition of the time,
Which cannot look more hideously upon me
Than I have drawn it in my fantasy.

Enter Lancaster, Clarence, Gloucester, Westmoreland, and others

Warwick: Here come the heavy issue of dead Harry:
O that the living Harry had the temper
Of him, the worst of these three gentlemen!
How many nobles then should hold their places
That must strike sail to spirits of vile sort!

Lord Chief-Justice: O God, I fear all will be overturn'd!

Lancaster: Good morrow, cousin Warwick, good morrow.

Gloucester Clarence: Good morrow, cousin.

Lancaster: We meet like men that had forgot to speak.

Warwick: We do remember; but our argument
Is all too heavy to admit much talk.
Lancaster: Well, peace be with him that hath made us heavy.
Lord Chief-Justice: Peace be with us, lest we be heavier!
Gloucester: O, good my lord, you have lost a friend indeed;
And I dare swear you borrow not that face
Of seeming sorrow, it is sure your own.
Lancaster: Though no man be assured what grace to find,
You stand in coldest expectation:
I am the sorrier; would 'twere otherwise.
Clarence: Well, you must now speak Sir John Falstaff fair;
Which swims against your stream of quality.
Lord Chief-Justice: Sweet princes, what I did, I did in honour,
Led by the impartial conduct of my soul:
And never shall you see that I will beg
A ragged and forestall'd remission.
If truth and upright innocency fail me,
I'll to the king my master that is dead,
And tell him who hath sent me after him.
Warwick: Here comes the prince.

Enter King Henry V, attended

Lord Chief-Justice: Good morrow; and God save your majesty!
King Henry V: This new and gorgeous garment, majesty,
Sits not so easy on me as you think.
Brothers, you mix your sadness with some fear:
This is the English, not the Turkish court;
Not Amurath an Amurath succeeds,
But Harry Harry. Yet be sad, good brothers,
For, by my faith, it very well becomes you:

Sorrow so royally in you appears
That I will deeply put the fashion on
And wear it in my heart: why then, be sad;
But entertain no more of it, good brothers,
Than a joint burden laid upon us all.
For me, by heaven, I bid you be assured,
I'll be your father and your brother too;
Let me but bear your love, I 'll bear your cares:
Yet weep that Harry's dead; and so will I;
But Harry lives, that shall convert those tears
By number into hours of happiness.

Princes: We hope no other from your majesty.

King Henry V: You all look strangely on me: and you most;
You are, I think, assured I love you not.

Lord Chief-Justice: I am assured, if I be measured rightly,
Your majesty hath no just cause to hate me.

King Henry V: No!
How might a prince of my great hopes forget
So great indignities you laid upon me?
What! rate, rebuke, and roughly send to prison
The immediate heir of England! Was this easy?
May this be wash'd in Lethe, and forgotten?

Lord Chief-Justice: I then did use the person of your father;
The image of his power lay then in me:
And, in the administration of his law,
Whiles I was busy for the commonwealth,
Your highness pleased to forget my place,
The majesty and power of law and justice,
The image of the king whom I presented,
And struck me in my very seat of judgment;

Whereon, as an offender to your father,
I gave bold way to my authority
And did commit you. If the deed were ill,
Be you contented, wearing now the garland,
To have a son set your decrees at nought,
To pluck down justice from your awful bench,
To trip the course of law and Blunt the sword
That guards the peace and safety of your person;
Nay, more, to spurn at your most royal image
And mock your workings in a second body.
Question your royal thoughts, make the case yours;
Be now the father and propose a son,
Hear your own dignity so much profaned,
See your most dreadful laws so loosely slighted,
Behold yourself so by a son disdain'd;
And then imagine me taking your part
And in your power soft silencing your son:
After this cold considerance, sentence me;
And, as you are a king, speak in your state
What I have done that misbecame my place,
My person, or my liege's sovereignty.

King Henry V: You are right, justice, and you weigh this well;
Therefore still bear the balance and the sword:
And I do wish your honours may increase,
Till you do live to see a son of mine
Offend you and obey you, as I did.
So shall I live to speak my father's words:
'Happy am I, that have a man so bold,
That dares do justice on my proper son;
And not less happy, having such a son,

That would deliver up his greatness so
Into the hands of justice.' You did commit me:
For which, I do commit into your hand
The unstained sword that you have used to bear;
With this remembrance, that you use the same
With the like bold, just and impartial spirit
As you have done 'gainst me. There is my hand.
You shall be as a father to my youth:
My voice shall sound as you do prompt mine ear,
And I will stoop and humble my intents
To your well-practised wise directions.
And, princes all, believe me, I beseech you;
My father is gone wild into his grave,
For in his tomb lie my affections;
And with his spirit sadly I survive,
To mock the expectation of the world,
To frustrate prophecies and to raze out
Rotten opinion, who hath writ me down
After my seeming. The tide of blood in me
Hath proudly flow'd in vanity till now:
Now doth it turn and ebb back to the sea,
Where it shall mingle with the state of floods
And flow henceforth in formal majesty.
Now call we our high court of parliament:
And let us choose such limbs of noble counsel,
That the great body of our state may go
In equal rank with the best govern'd nation;
That war, or peace, or both at once, may be
As things acquainted and familiar to us;
In which you, father, shall have foremost hand.

Our coronation done, we will accite,
As I before remember'd, all our state:
And, God consigning to my good intents,
No prince nor peer shall have just cause to say,
God shorten Harry's happy life one day!

Exeunt

SCENE III

Gloucestershire. Shallow's orchard

Enter Falstaff, Shallow, Silence, Davy, Bardolph, and the Page

Shallow: Nay, you shall see my orchard, where, in an arbour, we will eat a last year's pippin of my own graffing, with a dish of caraways, and so forth: come, cousin Silence: and then to bed.

Falstaff: 'Fore God, you have here a goodly dwelling and a rich.

Shallow: Barren, barren, barren; beggars all, beggars all, Sir John: marry, good air. Spread, Davy; spread, Davy; well said, Davy.

Falstaff: This Davy serves you for good uses; he is your serving-man and your husband.

Shallow: A good varlet, a good varlet, a very good varlet, Sir John: by the mass, I have drunk too much sack at supper: a good varlet. Now sit down, now sit down: come, cousin.

Silence: Ah, sirrah! quoth-a, we shall
Do nothing but eat, and make good cheer,

Singing

And praise God for the merry year;
When flesh is cheap and females dear,
And lusty lads roam here and there
So merrily,
And ever among so merrily.

Falstaff: There's a merry heart! Good Master Silence, I'll give you a health for that anon.

Shallow: Give Master Bardolph some wine, Davy.

Davy: Sweet sir, sit; I'll be with you anon. most sweet
sir, sit. Master page, good master page, sit.
Proface! What you want in meat, we'll have in drink:
but you must bear; the heart's all.

Exit

Shallow: Be merry, Master Bardolph; and, my little soldier
there, be merry.

Silence: Be merry, be merry, my wife has all;

Singing

For women are shrews, both short and tall:
'Tis merry in hall when beards wag all,
And welcome merry Shrove-tide.
Be merry, be merry.

Falstaff: I did not think Master Silence had been a man of
this mettle.

Silence: Who, I? I have been merry twice and once ere now.

Re-enter Davy

Davy: There's a dish of leather-coats for you.

To Bardolph

Shallow: Davy!

Davy: Your worship! I'll be with you straight.

To Bardolph

A cup of wine, sir?

Silence: A cup of wine that's brisk and fine,

Singing

And drink unto the leman mine;
And a merry heart lives long-a.

Falstaff: Well said, Master Silence.

Silence: An we shall be merry, now comes in the sweet o' the night.

Falstaff: Health and long life to you, Master Silence.

Silence: Fill the cup, and let it come;

Singing

I'll pledge you a mile to the bottom.

Shallow: Honest Bardolph, welcome: if thou wantest any thing, and wilt not call, beshrew thy heart.
Welcome, my little tiny thief.

To the Page

And welcome indeed too. I'll drink to Master Bardolph, and to all the cavaleros about London.

Davy: I hope to see London once ere I die.

Bardolph: An I might see you there, Davy,-

Shallow: By the mass, you'll crack a quart together, ha!
Will you not, Master Bardolph?

Bardolph: Yea, sir, in a pottle-pot.

Shallow: By God's liggens, I thank thee: the knave will stick by thee, I can assure thee that. A' will not out; he is true bred.

Bardolph: And I'll stick by him, sir.

Shallow: Why, there spoke a king. Lack nothing: be merry.

Knocking within

Look who's at door there, ho! who knocks?

Exit Davy

Falstaff: Why, now you have done me right.

To Silence, seeing him take off a bumper

Silence *[Singing]*: Do me right,
And dub me knight: Samingo.
Is't not so?

Falstaff: 'Tis so.

Silence: Is't so? Why then, say an old man can do somewhat.

Re-enter Davy

Davy: An't please your worship, there's one Pistol come from the court with news.

Falstaff: From the court! let him come in.

Enter Pistol

How now, Pistol!

Pistol: Sir John, God save you!

Falstaff: What wind blew you hither, Pistol?

Pistol: Not the ill wind which blows no man to good. Sweet knight, thou art now one of the greatest men in this realm.

Silence: By'r lady, I think a' be, but goodman Puff of Barson.

Pistol: Puff!
Puff in thy teeth, most recreant coward base!
Sir John, I am thy Pistol and thy friend,
And helter-skelter have I rode to thee,
And tidings do I bring and lucky joys
And golden times and happy news of price.

Falstaff: I pray thee now, deliver them like a man of this world.

Pistol: A foutre for the world and worldlings base!
I speak of Africa and golden joys.

Falstaff: O base Assyrian knight, what is thy news?
Let King Cophetua know the truth thereof.

Silence: And Robin Hood, Scarlet, and John.

Singing

Pistol: Shall dunghill curs confront the Helicons?
And shall good news be baffled?

	Then, Pistol, lay thy head in Furies' lap.
Silence:	Honest gentleman, I know not your breeding.
Pistol:	Why then, lament therefore.
Shallow:	Give me pardon, sir: if, sir, you come with news from the court, I take it there's but two ways, either to utter them, or to conceal them. I am, sir, under the king, in some authority.
Pistol:	Under which king, Besonian? speak, or die.
Shallow:	Under King Harry.
Pistol:	Harry the Fourth? or Fifth?
Shallow:	Harry the Fourth.
Pistol:	A foutre for thine office! Sir John, thy tender lambkin now is king; Harry the Fifth's the man. I speak the truth: When Pistol lies, do this; and fig me, like The bragging Spaniard.
Falstaff:	What, is the old king dead?
Pistol:	As nail in door: the things I speak are just.
Falstaff:	Away, Bardolph! saddle my horse. Master Robert Shallow, choose what office thou wilt in the land, 'tis thine. Pistol, I will double-charge thee with dignities.
Bardolph:	O joyful day! I would not take a knighthood for my fortune.
Pistol:	What! I do bring good news.
Falstaff:	Carry Master Silence to bed. Master Shallow, my Lord Shallow,- be what thou wilt; I am fortune's steward- get on thy boots: we'll ride all night. O sweet Pistol! Away, Bardolph!

Exit Bardolph

Come, Pistol, utter more to me; and withal devise something to do thyself good. Boot, boot, Master Shallow: I know the young king is sick for me. Let us take any man's horses; the laws of England are at my commandment. Blessed are they that have been my friends; and woe to my Lord Chief-Justice!

Pistol: Let vultures vile seize on his lungs also!
'Where is the life that late I led?' say they:
Why, here it is; welcome these pleasant days!

Exeunt

SCENE IV

London. A street

Enter Beadles, dragging in Hostess Quickly and Doll Tearsheet

Hostess Quickly: No, thou arrant knave; I would to God that I might die, that I might have thee hanged: thou hast drawn my shoulder out of joint.

First Beadle: The constables have delivered her over to me; and she shall have whipping-cheer enough, I warrant her: there hath been a man or two lately killed about her.

Doll Tearsheet: Nut-hook, nut-hook, you lie. Come on; I 'll tell thee what, thou damned tripe-visaged rascal, an the child I now go with do miscarry, thou wert better thou hadst struck thy mother, thou paper-faced villain.

Hostess Quickly: O the Lord, that Sir John were come! he would make this a bloody day to somebody. But I pray God the fruit of her womb miscarry!

First Beadle: If it do, you shall have a dozen of cushions again; you have but eleven now. Come, I charge you both go with me; for the man is dead that you and Pistol beat amongst you.

Doll Tearsheet: I'll tell you what, you thin man in a censer, I will have you as soundly swinged for this,- you blue-bottle rogue, you filthy famished correctioner, if you be not swinged, I'll forswear half-kirtles.

First Beadle: Come, come, you she knight-errant, come.

Hostess Quickly: O God, that right should thus overcome might!
Well, of sufferance comes ease.

Doll Tearsheet: Come, you rogue, come; bring me to a justice.

Hostess Quickly: Ay, come, you starved blood-hound.

Doll Tearsheet: Goodman death, goodman bones!

Hostess Quickly: Thou atomy, thou!

Doll Tearsheet: Come, you thin thing; come you rascal.

First Beadle: Very well.

Exeunt

SCENE V

A public place near Westminster Abbey

Enter two Grooms, strewing rushes

First Groom: More rushes, more rushes.

Second Groom: The trumpets have sounded twice.

First Groom: 'Twill be two o'clock ere they come from the coronation: dispatch, dispatch.

Exeunt

Enter Falstaff, Shallow, Pistol, Bardolph, and Page

Falstaff: Stand here by me, Master Robert Shallow; I will make the king do you grace: I will leer upon him as a' comes by; and do but mark the countenance that he will give me.

Pistol: God bless thy lungs, good knight.

Falstaff: Come here, Pistol; stand behind me. O, if I had had time to have made new liveries, I would have bestowed the thousand pound I borrowed of you. But 'tis no matter; this poor show doth better: this doth infer the zeal I had to see him.

Shallow: It doth so.

Falstaff: It shows my earnestness of affection,-

Shallow: It doth so.

Falstaff: My devotion,-

Shallow: It doth, it doth, it doth.

Falstaff: As it were, to ride day and night; and not to deliberate, not to remember, not to have patience to shift me,-

Shallow: It is best, certain.

Falstaff: But to stand stained with travel, and sweating with desire to see him; thinking of nothing else, putting all affairs else in oblivion, as if there were nothing else to be done but to see him.

Pistol: 'Tis 'semper idem,' for 'obsque hoc nihil est:'
'tis all in every part.

Shallow: 'Tis so, indeed.

Pistol: My knight, I will inflame thy noble liver,
And make thee rage.
Thy Doll, and Helen of thy noble thoughts,
Is in base durance and contagious prison;
Haled thither
By most mechanical and dirty hand:
Rouse up revenge from ebon den with fell
Alecto's snake,
For Doll is in. Pistol speaks nought but truth.

Falstaff: I will deliver her.

Shouts within, and the trumpets sound

Pistol: There roar'd the sea, and trumpet-clangor sounds.

Enter King Henry V and his train, the Lord Chief-Justice among them

Falstaff: God save thy grace, King Hal! my royal Hal!

Pistol: The heavens thee guard and keep, most royal imp of fame!

Falstaff: God save thee, my sweet boy!

King Henry V: My Lord Chief-Justice, speak to that vain man.

Lord Chief-Justice: Have you your wits? know you what 'tis to speak?

Falstaff: My king! my Jove! I speak to thee, my heart!

King Henry V: I know thee not, old man: fall to thy prayers;
How ill white hairs become a fool and jester!
I have long dream'd of such a kind of man,
So surfeit-swell'd, so old and so profane;

But, being awaked, I do despise my dream.
Make less thy body hence, and more thy grace;
Leave gormandizing; know the grave doth gape
For thee thrice wider than for other men.
Reply not to me with a fool-born jest:
Presume not that I am the thing I was;
For God doth know, so shall the world perceive,
That I have turn'd away my former self;
So will I those that kept me company.
When thou dost hear I am as I have been,
Approach me, and thou shalt be as thou wast,
The tutor and the feeder of my riots:
Till then, I banish thee, on pain of death,
As I have done the rest of my misleaders,
Not to come near our person by ten mile.
For competence of life I will allow you,
That lack of means enforce you not to evil:
And, as we hear you do reform yourselves,
We will, according to your strengths and qualities,
Give you advancement. Be it your charge, my Lord,
To see perform'd the tenor of our word. Set on.

Exeunt King Henry V, & c

Falstaff: Master Shallow, I owe you a thousand pound.

Shallow: Yea, marry, Sir John; which I beseech you to let me have home with me.

Falstaff: That can hardly be, Master Shallow. Do not you grieve at this; I shall be sent for in private to him: look you, he must seem thus to the world: fear not your advancements; I will be the man yet that shall make you great.

Shallow: I cannot well perceive how, unless you should give me your doublet and stuff me out with straw. I beseech you, good Sir John, let me have five hundred of my thousand.

Falstaff: Sir, I will be as good as my word: this that you heard was but a colour.

Shallow: A colour that I fear you will die in, Sir John.

Falstaff: Fear no colours: go with me to dinner: come, Lieutenant Pistol; come, Bardolph: I shall be sent for soon at night.

Re-enter Prince John of Lancaster, the Lord Chief-Justice; Officers with them

Lord Chief-Justice: Go, carry Sir John Falstaff to the Fleet:
Take all his company along with him.

Falstaff: My Lord, my lord,-

Lord Chief-Justice: I cannot now speak: I will hear you soon.
Take them away.

Pistol: Si fortune me tormenta, spero contenta.

Exeunt all but Prince John and the Lord Chief-Justice.

Lancaster: I like this fair proceeding of the king's:
He hath intent his wonted followers
Shall all be very well provided for;
But all are banish'd till their conversations
Appear more wise and modest to the world.

Lord Chief-Justice: And so they are.

Lancaster: The king hath call'd his parliament, my lord.

Lord Chief-Justice: He hath.

Lancaster: I will lay odds that, ere this year expire,
We bear our civil swords and native fire
As far as France: I beard a bird so sing,
Whose music, to my thinking, pleased the king.
Come, will you hence?

Exeunt

EPILOGUE

Spoken by a Dancer

First my fear; then my courtesy; last my speech.
My fear is, your displeasure; my courtesy, my duty;
and my speech, to beg your pardons. If you look
for a good speech now, you undo me: for what I have
to say is of mine own making; and what indeed I
should say will, I doubt, prove mine own marring.
But to the purpose, and so to the venture. Be it
known to you, as it is very well, I was lately here
in the end of a displeasing play, to pray your
patience for it and to promise you a better. I
meant indeed to pay you with this; which, if like an
ill venture it come unluckily home, I break, and
you, my gentle creditors, lose. Here I promised you
I would be and here I commit my body to your
mercies: bate me some and I will pay you some and,
as most debtors do, promise you infinitely.
If my tongue cannot entreat you to acquit me, will
you command me to use my legs? and yet that were but
light payment, to dance out of your debt. But a
good conscience will make any possible satisfaction,
and so would I. All the gentlewomen here have
forgiven me: if the gentlemen will not, then the
gentlemen do not agree with the gentlewomen, which
was never seen before in such an assembly.
One word more, I beseech you. If you be not too

much cloyed with fat meat, our humble author will continue the story, with Sir John in it, and make you merry with fair Katharine of France: where, for any thing I know, Falstaff shall die of a sweat, unless already a' be killed with your hard opinions; for Oldcastle died a martyr, and this is not the man. My tongue is weary; when my legs are too, I will bid you good night: and so kneel down before you; but, indeed, to pray for the queen.